IF YOU [ ]:
FABULA, FANTASY,
F**KERY, HOPE

ALSO BY COLIN FLEMING

The Anglerfish Comedy Troupe

IF YOU [ ]: FABULA, FANTASY, F**KERY, HOPE

COLIN FLEMING

DZANC BOOKS

DZANC BOOKS

2580 Craig Rd.
Ann Arbor, MI 48103
www.dzancbooks.org

Library of Congress Cataloging-in-Publication Data Available on Request

First US edition: January 2022
Interior design by Michelle Dotter
Cover artwork by Matt Revert

"Brackets"--PEN America
"Blinkered"--AGNI
"My Death Tie"--The Ampersand Review
"Analogues"--The Hopkins Review
Sequentials--Conjunctions
"A Deuce Cross"--AGNI
"Red Sweatpants"--The Literary Review
"Junction Regale"--TriQuarterly
"One-Way Zebra"--The Massachusetts Review
"Rimer's Boots"--Bull
"Laying Sheets"--Boulevard

Printed in the United States of America

10   9   8   7   6   5   4   3   2   1

CONTENTS

To Dan

IF YOU [ ]

BRACKETS

principles—get them in order; best when moving forward in relationship
bait the traps; no one likes a verminy apt.
buy paint and spackle; what is an artist without supplies?
+ floor cleaner, bug spray
pesto, oregano, garlic—dinner "bounceback" from friday's argument
(she will thrill to it)
threesome—bad joke; explain leave her to heaven ref. and how i was
not saying she was crazy like gene tierney but that eyes betrayed roil-
ing inner beauty, etc. etc., make this fly
conciliatory notes (in study?) (why are the notes always getting lost?
come up with better storage plan)
need more plasticine—loads for the statuary tribute, which now will
have an apologetic quality

***

There are better ways to be made a fool of, of course. Wasn't technically a threesome, tho, due to my absence and that the third party
was uninvited. At least by me. Reserve dedication for plasticine series, of course. The statue would have been wasted on her anyway.
Funny when a little joke proves true. The Gene Tierney line was good

tho. Should use somewhere else. Will get round to one last flicker of attention. Monday, most likely, when more is in order. Parting letter. Official point of departure. Eternal farewell. I hereby take my leave. Need more traps. The rapscallions are now entering in droves. As though they have picked up on some personal weakness. A letting down of the guard. Very well. I shall leave the bodies of their fellows in the traps for a few days yet. A reminder to would-be encroachers. Don't forget: most of this is mental.

***

stratagem:
dear Jeanne, you and (troglodyte? Carbuncle-embossed? cretin?) should both
etc. etc. etc.
when i found his note in "our" book (hardbound matisse drawings I gave last year)
"conciliatory note" (???); should I? you never know; mistakes are made; but: the double-ended jelly dong; what the fuck; he didn't even look surprised when i walked in…
stop stop stop: have some pride man. close this door. had no idea tho she was into….apparati. or jobworths like that. tonight, we listen to "cranked up really high" at full volume; the closure process begins; read wagner libretto as well. he'd sic a dragon on their asses. hmmm. fanciful. grog flows freely. me likey. inspiration is like a bath. tip to toe when it comes. here ye. general outline of pod (point of departure) letter:
—apologies for the [ ], regards
for the [ ], if you really think i'm wrong,
if you [ ], you should [ ], but maybe there's

no point in knowing better ~~dinner date ref.~~
~~us you him me them them over there~~
plaster statue—just knock off the head
i forgot to get glue at the store but
glue wasn't going to etc. etc. etc. us here (work out metaphor)
just put it all together
and see what happens
it is not my place to tell you how
to [ ] or [ ]

BLINKERED

She was screaming *I hate you I hate you I never loved you* and I swear I just wanted her to stop yelling. She was kicking at me and I had my arm around her and there was blood because her lips were so dry, and when she bit me I pretended I was going to spit on her face like that would stop her. If she got me where she wanted to get me when she started kicking it would have been one and done. Me on the floor rolling around. Only she'd still be yelling and I'd have no control over what was happening.

When we're nearly done she starts on about her father while she's gasping for breath and how he's coming soon to do his glorious rescue. *He knows all about you,* she says. *The kind of ogre you are. And my brothers too.* One of them got smashed up in a wreck and the other used to grope her so I'm thinking they're not the most reliable allies—no more than the friends she invents. She used to say she didn't have any before me. Now it's that she doesn't have any because of me. Clever. Right from the start she'd use words like they were riddles coming out of nowhere. *Do you ever get manic?* she asked me at the beginning. *Do you ever get manic and want something to tear you or fill you? Just a little? Not for long but so it feels like your skin is coming undone and someone is getting in there?*

Getting in where, I asked, and her eyes went wild.

I don't say anything after a certain point because when I do she gets louder. And her jaw sticks out further if I try to go on. Even if I just take a quick breath and move my tongue to the top of my mouth. *Don't you dare cut me off,* she says. *You're not the only one who gets to do the talking.* She sticks her fingers in her mouth and bites into the edges of her nails so there's always dried blood. Sexy.

Absolutely anything can start it. Any little question I dream up: How was your day? Do anything today? Oh your dad called, did he. How's he been? She turns it all around fast. *You know I didn't do anything,* she says. Yeah I do. Because when I come in she's sitting there in the dark and you just know she's kept it dark all day. So I ask her what the problem is. *Don't call them problems,* she says. *They are issues. That's the word and you know it. Issues can be got through.* I tell her problems can be solved and her eyes go even wilder.

We always make sure to do something else once it's over. Then it's fine for a bit. Safe fine like no one wants to start it again so we get a little lull. She cleans up a bit and washes her hands and her face, and we go outside with her squinting because of the sun and her puffy eyes. In the spring she likes the ducks in the square. The same two come every year. She feeds them sometimes but usually the man from the art studio on the corner is there first and her face bunches up. Neither of us really says anything except nice little things that wouldn't bother anyone, like, *How's your brother?* or *What about the beach tomorrow?* though there's no way in hell we're going.

I think she works on her lines while we're out because she hardly says anything. Then later she's primed to go off again. *Answer me so help me,* she likes to say. *You are not even looking at me,* she says. *You are not even paying attention to me. I don't matter to you.* Lots of people live in this building, you know. They all have ears even if a lot of them are off to bed by the time we get around to it. She talks fast, one word one word one word boom boom like they're almost connected and getting louder. Then I look over my shoulder and wait for the doorknob to turn all in a spasm and then the first splinter when they kick it down like *this woman needs to be saved and let's go.* The police are like that. Like every drunk guy in every pub when he gets the chance to play hero.

No way the heroes would knock first. Not with her. Screaming. You this and that. *I jump through hoops for you. If anyone knew what I go through with you. Oh yeah this is what I wanted when I was a little girl, someone just like you.*

Please, I say. *Don't you know how loud you are? We can't do this in here.*

Oh I bet you'd like to get me somewhere alone where no one can hear me you monster. I hate you. You have taken everything from me—my friends my family my dreams my hopes everything everything everything.

I hope not. But I know she wouldn't believe me if I said so. And she'd think I was being sarcastic and it would only make her louder.

Write me a letter, she said a couple of times. At least a couple of times. *You can write me a letter.* I asked her what kind. *You know.* I asked her if I could just say it. *Write it,* she said. So I did. I said sorry for all the times it got out of control, and I said that her being loud wasn't an excuse for what sometimes happened as a result. She taped the thing in the downstairs hallway for everyone to read. All the people who hear us must have seen it because I don't get up early since I don't have to. And wouldn't you know, someone took it down and stuck it under my door with a note on building stationary. *This is a peaceful building. The next time we will notify the police.* I think a mall cop lives here since I always see the guy in his uniform, but he doesn't have a gun or anything though he does have a walkie-talkie and a holster for it. So maybe he's the crusader for justice. But the teenage kids downstairs have been peddling blues for an age, and it's not like he's ever felt a need to step in there. Even with half the town coming and going to get their drugs. Though you won't be reading about their latest sales on an advert taped up in the fucking foyer.

I used to believe in the lulls. That a lull would become something lasting. Neither of us really says anything during the lulls beyond asking what's good on television tonight or is there any margarine left. Then anything can start it up again. *Here's your food,* she says. *I got it today fresh at the market. The fish market. And you know how crowded that is on Fridays.* I guess I do. I ask her how her day was and she says, *You know.*

No tell me, I say. And then she starts to cry sometimes. But when I don't ask she gets angry.

You don't care, she says. *You never cared. No one cares.* She bites the skin around her nails and the blood starts. *I made your dinner,* she says. *Maybe I can at least do that right.* I tell her I wasn't trying to make some kind of comment about her. *You never are. You never are and you never will so help me. Have your fucking fish,* she says and sort of tosses a chunk of haddock on the plate and slides it so it falls in my lap. *It is just like you not to like it.*

She shrieks out her words and I try to cut her off. *You are louder than God,* I say. That makes her laugh. A mean laugh that goes on and on. I try to look at her but I am not good at it. I try to look at her and say something without really saying anything like *why did this have to happen* and *why do we have to do this.* She stares at me hard like she's making up her mind to do something. Then she tells me she hates the way I treat her. That I am an animal that keeps her away from any kind of peace in every possible way. *I want to go home,* she says and jumps on the bed. She hits herself in the head and screams. I put my hand over her mouth and she bites me and we fall to the floor. I used to keep an oven mitt under the bed but it didn't stop the sound. My father would—

Your father is not here now, I say.

Or John or Craig or Emily or Jane or Rodney they would—

You made those people up, I say.

I hate you, she says, and she's crying.

Of course you do, I tell her.

I hate you.

Under the covers the words seem to stay there. While her face is still wet and covered with her hair I watch her breathe with her nose down in the pillow. *Do you think it will ever get better?* she says. *Me I mean? And us too?*

I don't know, I say. *I guess so.*

Good, she says. *I'm sorry. Are you listening to me?*

Yes, I tell her. *I really am. We can talk about it tomorrow.*

You know I don't—

Yes of course, I say.

You know I would never—

Yes, I say.

Even though—

Yes even though, I tell her. Even though I can hardly tell her I hate myself for the things I do. It's not like I don't know.

And we're just there like pebbles in a brook, she says. *Or like apples off the back of a truck that no one finds again.*

YELLOW HAMMERS

In our house, it meant one of two things if someone called me "Dude": either we were having a huge family gathering, or my dad had something very serious to say.

You can usually find our dog, Paxton, a Jack Russell, in the study when my dad is home. He writes about jazz and goes around the country interviewing musicians for his books, and my mom teaches history at my middle school. Anywhere else in the house, Paxton gets up to no good, hiding keys and tearing sheets of tissue in these weirdly even strips like he's going to doggy crochet something later. But with my dad, amidst all of those records and concert posters, he lays on his back, stares at the ceiling fan, and sort of bops his head along to the music of Thelonious Monk.

"I wanted to talk to you, Dude, about a special little addition to our house in the next few days," he began, as *Thelonious in Action* played on the stereo, a staple of my dad's serious talks.

I looked down at Paxton.

"We're getting another dog? You always said we could have just one. We're not unloading Paxton, are we?"

"No. Nothing like that. But my friend from Florida, Doles Odom…you remember Doles, right?"

He was this genius pianist my dad would meet up with and follow around the South, doing interviews with him and recording his music.

"Well," my dad continued, "he's been sick, very sick, and, um, his boy, Leb, is going to stay with us for the rest of the school year and the summer, until his dad gets better. His mother is not really in the picture, and he asked me, as a special favor, and I'm asking you, as one for me, if he can bunk with you. As shipmates."

"What?"

"He'll be staying in your room. And I shouldn't tell you his dad is sick. You're getting too old for me not to give you the straight truth. He has a drug problem. A very bad drug problem. He's going somewhere for a cure. Do you understand?"

I thought I did, even if the cure bit sounded like you'd visit a magical spring or well. But I just said "sure" and "of course" and "when?" with that last word seeming to brighten my father, and Monk transitioned into one of his major key melodies.

"Fine," my dad said, "fine." A repeated word with my father generally meant he was proud.

We drove from our house in the Berkshires in Palmer, Massachusetts, to Boston to pick up Leb at Logan Airport. We were the same age, and I knew that he played baseball like me.

I was racking it up in Little League that year with my pitching. Even Masie, my seven-year-old sister/nemesis, realized that the cool thing to do was to go to Engone Field when I was pitching. I had thrown three no-hitters in a row.

"This is the first time I don't mind having you as a brother," she informed me.

"And why's that?"

"Because if I tell a boy that you and me are related, they want to talk more. Before, it was harder to get a conversation started."

"Glad I could help."

"But I still think you bite it otherwise."

"Okay, you."

Leb was quiet in the car, and I was too, because I figured I'd feel really weird in his position. He looked older than me. I was thin, but he was all muscle. Taut.

At the house, I carried his bags into my room, though I think he could have carried them in one hand if he wanted to and probably would have preferred me not helping even if he would have done the same thing. He came in a second later and started smiling when he saw all of my baseball posters.

"I take it you play?" he said.

I told him I did, and that I pitched.

"I pitch a little, too."

You could tell from the way he said it that he did more than pitch a little.

As I was starting to ask him if he was any good, he began to wheeze like crazy. The nerves of being uprooted, I didn't know. He pulled this inhaler from his pocket and brought it to his lips.

"Jesus. Are you okay? Want me to get my dad?"

His face got all puffy, like one of those fish I'd see on summer vacation at the Cape that pump themselves up like balloons.

"Just…give…me…a…"

"Point at the ceiling if you're dying, and I'll call 911."

Not my most calming statement ever, but expeditious enough. There'd been a woman who had died alone in our house before we lived there, or that's what Masie said. She researched grim shit. "It's good that she croaked—makes it less likely that we will. Houses usually only have so many deaths." My sister liked to play percentages.

Leb took three quick hits on the inhaler and the puffiness went away and he was fine again. Just like that. The death metrics of the house remained where they were.

"I can't run very far. I can't run the bases when I play ball. I just pitch."

"They let you just pitch?"

"Yeah. They let me just pitch."

I got the sense that this might be a problem. He sounded like he knew exactly how good he was.

My dad liked to say that not a lot of people knew exactly how good they were. The ones who did were the ones that nobody else could touch.

"How hard do you throw?"

"About seventy-two miles an hour."

"Christ. And you just blow it by hitters?" Admittedly, this seemed obvious, but already I knew he was one of those kids who were likely to have that "more," the extra bit when they already had stuff that other kids didn't.

"Sure. But I have a curve. That's the sort of mean one. Dude."

I liked that he had picked up on our little tradition already. My dad had called each of us that a few times in the car. He worked us all in. Leb got as many dudes thrown his way as I did.

"I don't call your dad Dude back, do I?"

"Ha. No."

"Should I call him Uncle Whitey? Because there probably aren't a lot of other blacks in Palmer, right?"

"Yes. But no. That's not what I mean. Although he'd probably think it was funny."

"Fair enough, Julian."

"Everyone calls me Jules."

"Fair enough, Jules. 'Jules Tagellen taking the mound.'" He did a very regal announcer voice. A kingly announcer. "Looking forward to seeing you throw."

"You too. You really throw seventy-two?"

"Yeah. But the curve's the mean one."

***

He was right about that—it was the mean one.

My best friend Sean Kessler, whom everyone called Kessel, faced Leb before I did in Little League after the Brickhouse Pizzeria Athletics got first dibs to pick him because they had the worst team in the league.

"You are so not going to want to face this guy, Jules."

"And why's that?"

"Um, because of fucking everything? The ball is a blur with his fastball. Like some super-sped-up snowflake coming at you that melts. It looks more like light than a ball. I was terrified he was going to hit me. But then he has this curve. It starts off like it's coming from behind you, might maybe even miss the backstop, and you start to relax. You think it slipped out of his hand. Then it changes direction in midair, cuts in front of your chest, drops down at your knees, and the umpire yells strike. I almost fell over. You can't make a Wiffle ball move like that. I told my dad later, and he started laughing. Said in his day that was a called a yellow hammer, a big, monster, suck your balls back into your stomach, curve like that. When I had to go up to face him again, all I could think was, 'I really don't want to be doing this right now.'"

"He doesn't run though, right?"

"No. Poor kid. With his dad being on that crystal meth and all..."

"I never said that."

"Well what do you think it was?"

"I don't know."

"You didn't ask him?"

"He's been here like two weeks. Most of the time he's sad. I'd be sad. You'd be sad. He likes Masie. He helps her with her homework. I think he's probably smarter than us."

"You need to see this hammer thing anyway. Someone should do a science project on it."

Kessel wasn't always the best news source. Some guys tell stories, but Kessek tended to supersize his.

Everything was dramatic with Kessel. We had to look at some rocks in science class, and sure enough, Kessel cuts his finger open on a piece of obsidian and starts screaming like he's bleeding out. He missed the next three periods. He's what my mom calls girthy and what Masie calls fat. It's never bothered him, though. Doesn't stop girls from liking him either. He even has this line he does.

"Just baby fat, Jules. It'll grow away. In the meanwhile, I'm just sporting a little chunk, if you know what I mean. And if you extra know what I mean."

A clown, but he probably thought I was an equal clown, or we wouldn't have been best friends.

I wasn't at Leb's first Little League game because I had my paper route, and when this was done I liked to stop at Quincey Wicks's house because I figured someday I was going to marry Quincey. No one knew this. Kessel could probably pick up on some things, but I never said anything directly.

Quince and I had a complicated relationship. Her mom was this former Olympic swimmer, and she took me to swimming lessons with Quincey and these other two girls, Kelly Jackson and Elizabeth Hartman, who later moved away.

I guess her mom wanted to keep an eye on me and I was too little to go into the boys' shower by myself, so she brought me into the one the girls used. I made the mistake of telling Kessel this.

"Kid, that is so wrong. You looking at girls that age."

"I was that age too."

"That doesn't matter. I think you have to register for things now."

"I don't have to register for things. You...you..."

"What?"

"You look like Grimace. The McDonald's guy. You're shaped like Grimace."

But Kessel didn't care. You couldn't budge him in what he thought about himself. I envied him that way.

Later Quincey was coming home with her mom and she didn't have a seatbelt on. Her mom was one of those moms who wouldn't make you wear one, and when she stopped short she'd shoot her arm out to cover whoever was in the front. Like that would be enough.

Quincey went through the windshield and was in a coma for two weeks. That was in sixth grade. Someone would always sit next to the bed in the hospital. I told my dad I wanted to help and he talked about it with my mom and when Mrs. Wicks had to work or no one else could be there, I would sit with Quincey, hoping she'd wake up and see me first, but way more than that just begging God she'd wake up at all.

I wasn't there when she did, but it was still a while until she went home, and then she stayed there for some indefinite period. I guess I say "indefinite" because I measured in relation to me, what I knew, though I'm sure a plan was in place. You couldn't be loud around her. She was quieter than before, too. That's when I started coming around after school. I'd bring her homework and we'd play Monopoly and eat pudding cups her mom brought up to her room. The one time we kissed was after I had landed in Monopoly jail, which always cracked her up. I could taste the chocolate from the pudding. She said thank you after. I didn't know what that meant.

We didn't kiss again. I figured we would later, once other things sucked less or sucked clearer, to use a line of Kessel's, which I think was supposed to be funny or wise or sexual or a rich combo.

"Hitting a round ball with a round bat is a matter of timing," I wrote in a paper for science class. Me forcing matters, paper-wise.

Any excuse to get baseball in there, and any excuse, too, at that point, to sort of stick my hand up and wave it around, as if to say that I knew nothing was ever so simple as baseball when you can't even find the words to give name to the things you're starting to care about more. I was starting to feel like I was both on to something and totally floundering. "So is life," I added to the sentence about hitting being a matter of timing.

I got an A on that one. I thought of that as my Quince paper. Not that I titled it that, obviously. It was mostly bullshit but it also wasn't. It was combo-ish.

***

Everything settled into a routine as spring went on.

Leb and I would talk at night in our beds. At first it was just baseball. We had faced each other quite a few times by then. I had only gotten a handful of hits off of him, but that was way more than anyone else.

He swatted some rockets off of me, but he had to have a stand-in runner, who stood near the on deck circle and would take off when Leb made contact.

We were the two best players in the league. Whomever was voted the annual Most Valuable Player had to partake in a Palmer tradition that went back decades, that tradition being Lash Lagreux Day. Lagreux was a Palmer pitcher who played briefly for the Red Sox and became a World War II hero on account of the food drops he'd make into France with the German artillery firing on him.

Every year, at the end of the season, the town would come out to Engone Field, and the Little League MVP would stand all alone in the middle of the outfield as this rusty-looking former Coast Guard cutter would fly overhead and drop an orange, which the MVP would try to catch.

No one ever really got close, but I figured until Leb came along I'd get a shot and if anyone could nab citrus fruit falling out of the clouds, it'd be me.

Leb would have a couple of breathing attacks each day. He kept his inhaler on the corner of the desk in my room, next to a CD his dad made which my dad told me was a modern classic called *She Sings in Colors*. Leb played it for me one night. I didn't know that piano music could be so beautiful. It was like someone talking to you. Someone, as I tried to explain to Kessel, who had your back.

"You are losing it, my friend, if you think jazz has your back. Metallica's *Black Album* has your back. Used it to pump myself up big time before yesterday's game."

"You went zero for five. I struck you out four times."

"Yeah but I felt pumped doing it."

I could live with Leb being better at a sport than I was. Sometimes there's such a gap between you and someone else in one area that is relevant, maybe even super important, to both your lives, that you're not all that threatened, they're just better. But you're also not threatened because you figure you'll make up that distance somewhere else, and so long as the thing in the first place isn't the single most important thing to you, you kind of wait for your moment elsewhere. You hover.

Quince was coming over a lot, too, with Leb there. She was our grade's star student, and she was sort of assigned to help Leb with his schoolwork. Not that he needed it. I think this was because of him coming in so late and all. The more she hung out over at our place, though, the more Leb would talk at night. And less about baseball.

"You can ask me about my dad, you know," he said to me one night as we did our shipmates routine, or bunkmates, whatever archaic terminology my dad used that day he had turned down the Monk LP so we could talk.

"I didn't want to be weird."

"Well, it's a little weird you haven't said anything, right, Dude?"

"Okay. Probably. Do you think he's going to be okay?"

"I do. My dad is strong. I'm not as strong as my dad. I don't know if I ever could be. I know it takes a lot for him to make his music, and he didn't get over my mom leaving. I was really young and I don't remember her much. But I know there was never any sign she was going to go. He thought we were happy. He's said that to me a few times. He tried everything he could to reach her when she left, but there was nothing ever again. Only lawyers. He poured everything into me and into writing his music. And he hasn't gotten the recognition he deserves. He worries he's running out of time. People like your dad are a big reason anyone knows his work at all. But he'll be back."

"My dad says he's a genius. Do you think an athlete can be a genius?"

"Not if you're a sprinter or a shot-putter. Then you just put your head down and go. But I think a pitcher can be brilliant, at least. The pitcher can control timing, tempo, comfort, trust even. That's more than most people can do. And a pitcher can always make sure that someone is held accountable. There isn't enough of that in this world. That was the last thing my dad said to me when he put me on that plane to come up here. 'Always hold a person accountable, Leb,' he said. 'Even if you don't want to. Even if it's harder. Even if that person is you.'"

He made me believe in the guy, junk or no junk. And doubt myself a little.

"Hey, Jules, what was that last pitch you threw me in my first at bat?"

"Little slider thingy I've been working on."

"You need to work on it some more. Throw it again and I'm going to park it over the scoreboard."

"Noted."

"Bring the heat. I still can't hit your heat yet."

"Okay."

"I said 'yet.'"

"I know."

***

Leb took the MVP honors, despite only being in Palmer for half the season. I had thrown three consecutive no-hitters, but he threw three straight perfect games, which was a state record.

"You must be ticked off, eh there superstar?" Kessel asked.

"No not really. He fanned your Grimace ass, what, fifteen times?"

"Every single time I faced him. I got that hit off you though."

"You popped out to second."

"I hit it is what I meant. And what I extra mean, if you catch my drift."

"Stop saying that 'extra mean' thing. It makes you sound crazy."

It was Masie who got me feeling crazy. She was even less reliable for news than Kessel, but still, you expect your flesh and blood to only go so far with a lie.

"Do you love Quincey?" she asked me one morning as I was trying to get down my breakfast burrito while Leb showered for school.

"What's going on now?"

"Because I think she loves Leb. I saw them…"

"You saw them what?"

"In the basement. When the TV was on. They were…"

"Don't fuck with me."

"Being…extra friends."

"What does that mean?"

"You know. Extra."

"Why are you rubbing your hands together? Extra friends like that? Good Christ. Tell me—"

"I have glue on them. This gets it off."

I looked under the table, where Paxton was ripping the face off of his Mr. Potato Head stuffed animal with some strips of ripped Kleenex sticking out from under what my mom always called his loin for some disturbing reason. I wanted to throw up.

I didn't say anything to Leb, but I tried to read some meaning in Quincey's eyes at school and then at home.

Nothing. Until Lash Lagreux Day, when Masie came out to the backyard where I was working on my swing.

It was a Saturday, but we had the final tests of the year the next week. Quincey was in the basement studying with Leb.

"They're doing the extra friend stuff, if you want to see."

"Guard the backyard."

"What does that mean?"

"It means stay here."

I went down the basement stairs as quietly as I could. There was a *Brady Bunch* rerun on TV. Leb and Quincey were on the couch. She was lying on her back with her head on his leg. They were holding hands.

So that's how we're doing this, I thought as I retreated back to my room.

Leb's inhaler was where it always was on the corner of his desk. One of the drawers was open as if to say, "Feed me, big boy." I took the inhaler, put it in, shut the drawer, and tried not to cry. I felt stupid and angry and tragic, like the people we read about in English, and confused. So confused. I even wondered if it would have mattered if I'd been the first one she saw when she woke up in the hospital. Catchers give signs, naturally, but maybe she would have looked at it like the Fates do, too. Not that Quincey cared fuck all about sports. I didn't think so, anyway.

I opened the drawer again a few inches so I wasn't doing anything too bad. Then I got on my bike and pedaled to Engone Field even though the ceremonies weren't starting for another four hours.

When they did, Leb wasn't there. Neither was my family. The commissioner said that, as the MVP runner-up, I'd have to stand in the outfield and try to catch the orange.

I watched as that orange came flying down. I could feel everyone's eyes on me. I took a few steps back, then a few to the side, and as I heard the whirl of the helicopter blades reverberating in my ears, I felt that orange hit me at the top of my nose, and I tasted blood.

Then there was nothing but this pervading wooz, and a blanketing, goodnight thought of "You had it coming, dick."

***

I knew my dad was in the ambulance with me. I could hear his voice as I passed in and out of consciousness. It was like being awake and asleep at the same time.

When I woke up for good, I was in a bed and no one was there. I don't know why I looked around hoping to see Quincey. Then I remembered Leb and what I had done. Something must have happened. I wondered if I had killed him, if he had some attack—maybe he was excited doing that extra stuff—and couldn't breathe and no one could find the inhaler to get him to breathe again. I got up and started to leave the room when my dad came in. He must have been in the bathroom or something.

"Whoa, Dude, where do you think you're going?"

"Dad?"

"You took quite a blow. On top of being dehydrated, the doctor said. He wants us to wait a few hours before checking you out."

"Leb...is he..."

"He went over Quincey's. Didn't want the attention, I guess. That's why we were late."

"Nothing happened to him?"

"Like what?"

"Nothing."

My dad looked at me kind of hard. I knew not to look away. Then he'd know I was lying. I was going to tell him. But it felt like math, like an order of operations things, if that makes any sense. Who you tell first matters more sometimes than who you tell second, so long as everyone who needs to know is going to know in the end.

Leb looked at me harder at dinner than my dad had. I slept down in the basement on the couch because I didn't want to face him before he could do what I knew was right for him to do, and what he would do. I also knew that he probably understood he had had enough of an impact on me that I was coming around to some of his rules, some of the ways he got through life. Maybe how his dad got through life. Maybe how I'd have to get through life someday. I didn't know. But I did know I'd be facing him the next day in the batter's box at the annual All-Star game.

I understood what was coming as I stepped up to the plate. I remembered what he said about accountability, so I just stood there with my eyes shut as he went into the windup for his first pitch.

He missed me. Then he missed me with a second pitch. The ball went past my ear with a sizzle to it that reminded me of dropping bacon on the grill during the winter, when my dad cooked outside even though it was twenty degrees. "Stand with me," my dad would say, tossing my coat out of the closet into my arms, like those winter grilling moments were tantamount to a rite of passage. Perhaps they were. Leb ran the count full, each pitch coming closer and closer. I almost wished for one of those big yellow hammers to drop down out of the sky and curve into the strike zone and buckle my knees such that I fell over and everyone laughed. But no—I knew he was bringing the gas. What I didn't know was that it was going to be right over the plate, and that I was going to throw myself into it, chipping my collar bone, some bone chunks drifting down into my lung, as it turned out, another ride back to the hospital with the same EMTs. "Rough week," one of them said, which I think was a joke.

I had to stay in the hospital for a couple days to make sure I didn't have trouble breathing, until those bone chips were absorbed into my system. Leb didn't visit, but I knew he wasn't keeping away. Just like I knew he hadn't tried to hit me. I had done that because of something I had done to him. And that was my way of making it right.

When we got home, I had a sling on, but I could still pedal my bike with one hand. I left for Quincey's house. My parents said Leb was there, but it wasn't like I needed them to tell me.

I sat outside on the curb for a couple hours, hoping Leb would see me and break off his extra stuff, if that's what he was doing. Sometimes you just know when there's no one in a house, but you have no real proof, it doesn't make sense that you know, so you sit there. Hope someone emerges. Someone you can't go looking for directly, so you just wait, and hope whatever you get from them, when they do emerge, is what they need, and what you need. I was thinking how that could be another science paper when Leb rode up on my dad's bike, his inhaler sticking out of his shirt pocket.

"She's not even home, Dude."

"No, I know. I've known for a while. Look, Leb—"

I didn't have a way to frame what I wanted to say. I wanted to say something about his dad, and how I made a mistake, too, but that a mistake that hurts someone you care about doesn't mean you don't care about them or that they're not teaching you what it means to care in that way you're going to have to try and care about everything that's going to be important in your life going forward. And they gave you that. And it wasn't just that you were sorry for being a total dick—it was that you didn't know how you'd repay them. Or maybe it was that you didn't know how you'd convey any of this.

"I think you should be with Quincey," I said. "I think she likes you a lot. You'd be good for each other. And she did a report for English class, before you got here, on Miles Davis. So, you know. Things in common."

"Why are you rubbing your hands together like that?"

"I have glue on them."

"No you don't."

"True. I'm just nervous. What do you say, Dude? Let me make it up to you."

I didn't expect to start crying in front of this guy. It wasn't something you did. When you got hit by a pitch, any pitch, no matter how fast, you were supposed to take your base and not even rub where you'd been hit. But there's a difference when you start to take a base together with someone else, which is a whole new weird thing you don't see coming until it is right there upon you.

"You remind me a bit of my dad," Leb said. "He got banged up a lot, too. But like he says, 'Being banged up can be a start.'"

"Start of what?"

"I don't know. Not being banged up again."

I told him I thought that was wise, and he told me he'd never seen anyone dive into a seventy-mile-per-hour fastball before.

"You were the real yellow hammer," he said, laughing as we started walking our bikes, while I thought, *No, Dude, that'd be you.*

MY DEATH TIE

Ever wonder what clothes you're going to be buried in? You probably haven't. Morbid, right? No one likes morbidity. Morbidity's a drag. Horror's cool. Scary films, Halloween, Bela Lugosi. But morbidity is a bring-down. How old are you? How many years, realistically, do you think you have left? See? A drag.

I've wondered what clothes I'm going to be buried in. Or, rather, I've worried that someone is going to screw up my last wishes—even though I've stated them well in advance, and printed out several written copies for my parents and my fiancée.

My great-aunt just died. The funeral made me pensive. At the cemetery, I wandered off. Found me a most impressive headstone. An open-ended headstone. There was a dead husband, with dates accounted for. Beginning and end. He had a wife, born in 1904. Died in—didn't say. Blank space after the dash. So, she's either out there, or her body's gone missing.

My fiancée had a different take on the matter, after she managed to find me.

"She probably died a long time ago and no one wanted to pay for the inscription. Or even to bury her. What time are we going to your aunt's?"

Morbid, right?

By aunt, she didn't mean my great-aunt, whom we'd just interred, but just a regular aunt hosting a post-funeral brunch. I don't know if you call it that. There were muffins.

I had a friend named Judd. Bad guy. Nonetheless, I was wearing a tie he once owned. He was friends with my better friend, Leonard. Good guy, if a little misguided. Leonard got me a painting gig with Judd. Room painting, not Van Gogh–type painting. He enjoyed having me fold the drop cloths, after we were finished, while he prowled around bedrooms in search of vibrators and assorted paraphernalia.

We weren't grown up then. But we are now. Leonard still knows Judd. I do not. Leonard impregnated his wife not too long ago, after the Patriots came from behind to defeat the Colts in thrilling fashion. "I was pumped up," Leonard said. He also told Judd about his wife being with child and Judd asked him if he could eat the afterbirth. Leonard declined, and also elected to pass on Judd's offer to pig roast his wife. "It's a lot of life activity, when you think about it," Leonard remarked, and I just responded, "Okay."

Anyway, Judd and I were painting, a bunch of years ago, near my aunt's house. The great dead one. She lived with my grandmother. My good one. Not my father's mother, who referred to me as a bastard.

"Well, technically, you are, aren't you?" my fiancée remarked on one of our first dates. Yes. I am. That is true. Still, I do think it was a bit much for my father's mother to declare "Blood will tell!" when my imminent adoption was announced. Blood will tell. I say it all the time now. It makes me feel like I'm in a Shakespeare play.

As it turned out, the regular aunt happened to there that day too. Dropping off prune juice, which was a service she provided for my great-aunt, who loved the stuff.

My great-aunt was pretty spinster-like. Not like you want to be brooding on hymens, but we were all pretty sure she was a virgin. No one—even the old timers—ever remembered her going on a date. She didn't like my good grandmother, who lived on the bottom floor of the house. When you visited my grandmother, she'd tell you to be quiet so my great-aunt wouldn't hear you and come down. You'd have to visit her before you left, but it was best to put this off as long as possible. (I did not give the eulogy.)

Judd and I stopped in, and there were the three of them downstairs. My prune-juice-toting aunt was just shy of middle age then. Pretty attractive. Judd started talking up a storm. I hardly said a word. I became nervous. I couldn't get a full breath until the visit came to an end and we were back in the car. And then Judd made a request.

"Why don't you do me a solid and go in there and hook me up with your aunt."

"The old virgin?"

"Nah, that cutie."

I mentioned she was married to my uncle.

"I'm cool with that."

We sat there arguing for ten minutes. It was a mercy when he finally put the car in gear.

He kept phoning me about his solid, though. I changed my phone number. I told Leonard I wanted nothing to do with this guy. I had to be stealthy. Leonard apprised me of some of Judd's late-night habits—useful, given that we lived a couple blocks from each other. For instance, he enjoyed showering at one thirty in the morning and heading out into the night, all alert, looking for the drunk women staggering home from the bars. One night I saw him going about his woman-hunting business and was forced to dive behind a dumpster, lest he see me.

"You're going to want to stay out of that alley by the all-night bakery," Leonard said.

"Why on earth would I be in the alley?"

"Judd goes in the alley."

"Jesus, man. Why would I be in the alley with Judd?"

People take all kinds of weird routes to get to the story they want to tell you. You can't just tell a story. It needs to be set up. Maybe there's a subtle sitcom influence in American conversation today. I don't know. As it turns out, Judd had coaxed a young lady onto her knees in this alley of dirty deeds. Needless to say, he mounted her from behind. But with a rather piquant flourish, he ordered her to "Look at the lights!" as the cars drove past.

I pointed out this alley and its singular backstory to my fiancée one night between mouthfuls of pizza that we munched down outside the bakery.

"Wow. That's messed up. He must be really handsome."

Disturbing. It is comments like this that make me think a re-think is in order, regarding said fiancée. Then again, it's been long enough, and everyone needs to pony up at some point and do the marriage deed. I probably won't put it that way to her.

The "look at the lights" episode was reprised, after a fashion, a few months later. This time, the setting was a room—specifically, a spot up against the wall, by the window, near where a few construction workers were working outside. The refrain du jour: "Tell them to work harder! Tell them to work harder!"

As I said, I do own a tie of Judd's. It's tied. Pre-tied. I don't know how to tie a tie. So, whenever someone dies, I wear it. It's my death tie. Bad things have happened if I'm in this tie. I told my fiancée about all of this in the bathroom on the morning of my great-aunt's funeral.

"If this was a film," she said, "there'd be a cut right now to you on your back in the casket with this same tie. That'd be some nice continuity."

What the hell. I told her then and there: cook me. Cook me the fuck up. I don't want the casket. I'm going to need as big a boost as possible, afterlife-wise, as I can get. I don't have the most sparkling CV for heaven, I've made a lot of mistakes, and I really don't want to be taking any Judd attire along with me to the interview. I started to cry. My fiancée told me that my aunt must have been very special.

"I'm serious. Either teach me how to tie a tie, or tie one for me, and let that be my new death tie. No. Forget it. I like the purity of the cooking thing. That's better. I don't want to feel confined, in case, I don't know, you wake up after a while. Cook me and scatter me."

"What's wrong with you?"

"I love you. This relationship just feels right. Look—I need you to do something else. If something bad—you know, fatal—happens to me. I need you to…I need you to do a shot of me. It's not some cannibalism thing. I'm just saying, if I go before my time, and you put some ashes in a Dixie cup with some water…you're a good person. You could do a shot of me. And I could live on, organically. I love you."

I've had worse moments. I was once part of a Judd pig roast. It's going to suck if God has video of that. I don't have a defense. I was lonely. I drink too much.

She stayed in the bathroom to fix her hair. I went out into the living room and called Leonard and got his voicemail. He'd met my aunt—both of them. I left him a message about the funeral. And the brunch. At which I did not last long. The reaper's scythe had got inside my head. I was sweating. My mother was staring hard at me. Like I was hiding drugs on my person.

"Why are you fidgeting so much?"

"I'm not fidgeting, Mom. I'm just hot."

"Yeah, babe, you are fidgeting," said the fiancée. "And you don't feel hot to me."

I thought of the one thing that Judd said before that pig roast/threesome of yore had commenced: "It's less of a mistake if more people are doing it."

I had a scone. It was actually pretty good, all things considered. I made a note to pick up scones more often, and then resolved to make a break for the door. When I was five feet short of the front porch, my cell phone rang. It was Leonard.

"Sorry about your aunt. So young. I'm not being crass, you know. That's not a Judd thing. She was just so young."

"That's not the dead one. She's here right now." She was. She'd caught us trying to leave on the sly. I had to give her a hug. "Actually, I'm wearing Judd's tie. So we're all sort of here together."

Not really. But as I'd told Leonard—while my fiancée and my living aunt competed for the most shocked, put-off expression in the room, given that I am bad at whispering when my anxiety kicks in—if my uncle's presence hadn't cocked things up, all of this might have gone very differently indeed.

"Circle of life, man," I added, trying to pretend I was wise.

"Yeah, circle of life. You watching the Pats game tonight?"

EAP AND ABE

The ghost of Abe Lincoln and the ghost of Edgar Allan Poe were friends. They were thought of, at first, as an odd couple. You'd see them passing through the arbor of the kingdom of the dead to stroll along the river, which was wide and peaceful. Everyone knew ghost Lincoln as Abe and nothing more, and ghost Poe as EAP.

Abe was tall and lean, and walked with a hitch, which allowed EAP, who was short and bowlegged, to keep perfect pace. They were drawn to each other because they both had their deaths—or, in the language of this place, their First Deaths (FD)—before their time.

"Say, EAP," Abe wondered aloud one day, as took their regular constitutional. "When was your FD again?"

"At forty, you rotter. Before what should have been the midpoint of my life. Didn't get to be no fucking hero. No big superhero like Abe. A few more years, a bit more time, hell, maybe a good publicist, and I wouldn't have had to count on the whole posthumous glory thing. Because the thing that sucks about that…"

Abe would laugh, and make a movement to pat his friend on the back, his ghost hand, passing through the whole of EAP's ghost chest. But it was the thought that counted. Also, smart ghosts like these tended to favor up-to-date vernacular from back in the land of the living. Keeps one young.

"Quite, quite," Abe would remark. "Let us speak, then, of the works you planned to write. Had your time not been so cruelly curtailed."

EAP enjoyed this to some degree. It was his favorite way to talk about himself. To get into the things he didn't do, that he might have done. That he told himself he'd do, back before his First Death, but which he kept putting off. Often he had been very down and could do little else but put things off.

"Okay, right. So, you know 'Cask of Amontillado'?"

"I know it with pleasure."

"So what I was going to do, after the alcoholic juggler guy is sealed up in the wall, well, I was going to kick things up a notch. Like, it's bad for him and scary that he's going to die in there, but he's drunk, there isn't much air, he goes fast. Could have been way worse. So I was going to have this monster that was already inside, this big half rat, half man thing, and he was eternal, and could give eternal life to someone he might torment. The idea being that he'd give eternal life to the drunk who had been sealed up in there by his enemy. And then it'd be the two of them in that horrible, rank space, no room to move, sealed up forever, together, this dude and the rat monster."

"Marrow-chilling."

"Thank you."

"You might experiment with that. When you write. When next you write."

Abe was referring to what happens after you die if you write well, as EAP could, and believe in what you've written. You put your ghostly hand to your ghostly parchment, and whatever you set down came to pass as well, if you truly believed in its completeness. You could write it, or someone, right into your life. Your death-life.

"I don't know," EAP cautioned, though he was rarely the cautious type. "I don't know if that's something it'd be wise to play around with. I've already been playing around with some recreational interests. They are keeping me quite busy."

"Are they assuaging any of your sorrows?"

Abe and EAP were also friends, it should be noted, on the basis of their respective depressions.

"Slightly. They're a bit titillating."

"Tell me more," Abe requested, being a bit of a voyeur.

"Soon. When next we stroll. For we have come to the final embankment already. We seem to be walking faster these days, Abe."

"That we are, EAP. A fist bump for you"—and their fists went through each other—"and we shall visit soon."

EAP was missing for what came to be, more or less, three days, though time was difficult to measure. When he next joined his friend, outside the arbor, he was haggard. Heavy shadows of smoke lay under his eyes. They walked mostly in silence, and at the last embankment, EAP, in some desperation, invited Abe back to his home.

"For I dare not say what I have experienced where it might be overheard," he declared. EAP was quite popular with his fellow ghosts, and when a group of them heard something particular gruesome or ribald emanate from his lips, chants of "EAP EAP EAP!" would go up and down the vapory streets. He wasn't in the mood today.

Once they had settled in at what the locals called chez EAP, the harried ghost began his tale.

"So, I'm back on the dating site, and I'm so fucking depressed at this point, and so horny, frankly, that I am just about done looking for anything real. Of substance. You meet one idiot after another, and if you can handle all of the ridiculous text speak, you still have to handle people who know nothing about anything and talk in the same six clichés. 'I can stay in or I can go out.' Wow. Massive fucking accomplishment. 'I love to Netflix and chill.' Do you know how many fucking idiots say that?"

"Um…a lot?"

"Yes, a fucking lot. So what is there for me? Learned, articulate, passionate, and craving—"

"Strange?"

"Hmmm. Yes, well, strange things I suppose, and also strange. At this point. So I just say shit like, 'Oh, you seem so interesting, and you're a bit submissive,' which usually gets them to further compliment themselves, and then go into how submissive they are, or want to be. Pretty failproof. What are you doing?"

"Making notes."

"Don't write down this next part."

"Okay…"

"So I'm talking to this one ghost woman. Smoking."

"Ha."

"I thought you'd like that. And she wants to film herself for me, showing me how she gets off. I'd been jerking myself for almost three days at that point, trying to stave off the sadness—"

"You must have coated the place."

"No. No release. I wanted to look forward to something. It can be very hard to have something to look forward to. Anyway, she says her fantasy is to have this daughter and Daddy thing going on. And I was a good writer, could I give her some ideas, and then she'd use them and film herself. I gave her the ideas, and she went with it.

"Let me tell you, it was so wrong and hot. She's there working herself, index finger on her ghost clit, but never really on it, more like she's itching something super fast. But she's saying things like, 'I know you and Mommy aren't getting along very well lately, Daddy. When I put my head up outside your door at night, I never hear those sounds I like to hear when I listen and touch myself in the hallway. I want to make you feel good if Mommy won't. Is that wrong? Can I give you this video as a test to see if you'd like me this way?

We don't have to tell anyone if you come into my room at night. In a way, I've been in your penis before—"

"Fucking hell."

"I know, right? 'And being on it and having it in me does seem kind of right.' And so forth. This was so hot that I busted out the EAPer."

"No!"

"I did. Truly."

EAP had written a story about a man obsessed with masturbation whose problem manifests itself in the form of a three-foot member—called the EAPer, in the story of the same name—that emanates from his person and ultimately kills him. Thus was the EAPer made real, and EAP would sometimes affix it to himself for maximum pleasure, when he was at his most depressed and it took that much for him to feel anything, which, in that context, wasn't that pleasurable after all.

"Can I borrow it again?" Abe asked.

"Sure. Next time you have your truck, we'll load it in the back."

"But why not say this on the streets? You'd get many EAP-tastic chants over this one."

"True. But it's because of what happened after. After the conclusion of my edge-fest, which left me suicidal—irony—I decided to write. And I wrote a story in which there was a woman this foul, but also brilliant, and kind, and funny, and stable. It's tough to get all of that in one person. And because I wrote it, and I believed in her fully, she came out into the world. But I also didn't write enough. So there were other things, too. Which I hadn't counted on. And I was already struggling with the memories."

That was almost always a problem with these writing efforts. What one created sprang into being and was actual, but along with that came everything from before that person had been written. Prior memories, joys, hurts, hopes, dreams, dashed dreams.

"Where is she?" Abe asked. "Is she here now? Can I have a go?"

He was trying to be funny and inject some lightness into the situation, but his joke missed the mark. He put his ghost hand through EAP's ghost knee.

"No, she's not. She was all of those things, but, of course, there was the problem of what she had told me long ago, which I now knew, that she would leave at some point, probably with no warning, because as I am sad, she was sadder still, and while there is much I can face, if I drink enough, there is less she could face. I didn't really know how to end the story, so I picked it up later, and I hung myself from a bridge. So that's on my to-do list now."

"Well, that's easy enough. We can get that out of the way no problem."

EAP and Abe went down to the river again. Atop the bridge, a smoke-vine was passed over EAP's head. He saluted Abe and jumped toward the water. The smoke wouldn't hold, and thus he didn't jerk back up and start to bounce, as with a standard gibbeting.

He stood up, and shrugged his shoulders.

"Well, that didn't work."

Abe had some experience in these matters, having successfully hanged himself from the bridge many times, something he'd never shared even with EAP, so great was his own sadness that the idea of moving his vaporous lips on the subject had him contemplating the next leap riverward.

Abe had a can of vapor. When you sprayed vapor with vapor, the new vapor made the first vapor hard, solid, unbreakable. Some spray was applied to the mist-vine around EAP's neck, a salute was made, EAP jumped, and this time he died again. It was agonizing, but only in a physical way, which was, he thought, as his neck snapped, more preferable than other ways.

A few days later, Abe came by EAP's place to return the EAPer.

"Hey, Abe."

"What's up, EAP?"

"You all EAPed out?"

"You might say that. Doing all right since the latest death?"

"Guess so."

"How many is that now?"

"Don't know. Everything blends."

"Too much rain outside to walk, probably. We could try our hands at writing a story together until it clears. Didn't you wish to add onto 'The Raven' and have a part two, where Satan emerges from hell to protest the copyright over the poem, saying that he wrote it himself one evening in his Fiery Kingdom? That could be good."

"I don't know if we want to bring another devil into things."

"True, my friend. We could just sit and work the EAPer. It's out in the truck."

"I really should clean it."

"Well, let's take it to the car wash. You we can grab a bite after. You up for a bite?"

"Yeah, I could eat."

"Okay. Cool."

ANALOGUES

So much for shifts. That was our plan, like we were on a stakeout or something. But my wife, because she is my wife, is home sick in bed. She's supposed to be here tonight. Last night was my turn, and I was here. Right here. Same as now. I never even lost my couch. My father did not have a couch when he was doing this with my mother because he was bedside. I am officially waiting to visit. I never asked my father what his time was like because he would have just stared at me, and I think you can practically choke on those kinds of looks.

I have not and won't call to ask my wife just how sick she thinks she is. I cannot use the laugh. Hardly anyone says anything except if they whisper. Some people try and sleep the whole time. I watch the television. You can watch one show turn into another and sometimes you don't even know they're different. I like the commercials, when there's a bunch in a row and you look at the clock on the wall and see that the next show is about to start. It only took a day or two to memorize all the magazines. I can almost get sick off them now. They don't have any medical ones. Which you think would be relevant.

There's some coloring books on the table with everything else, even though hardly any kids come in here. I've only seen the two that were here yesterday. They sat at the table by the vending machine and didn't say a word, just colored. I do not know why I was watching.

Like their parents couldn't have left them at home. Kids scribbling their cards and writing Get Well like that's all anyone has to do and Grandma or some younger tragic case is going to get better. Just dry your eyes, love. Stroke it, children. I could never think like that. The rooms in here must be covered with little hopscotch drawings and smiley faces. Our kids are in school. Thank God. We just aborted one of them. Right here in this same place. It was down a floor. One of the pamphlets they had downstairs at the nurses' station was nice enough to tell me that there is love even in loss.

I've read every magazine here, and I won't watch the news. It's on at least six times a day. Come and get it. Another helping of news that never changes. It just gets rebroadcast. You should have heard that doctor, though. "She's going to be extra emotional," he said. "For I don't rightly know how long." That rightly. Like he had just come out of someone's barn. When he said what he did, I swear I thought he was talking about one of those vacuum cleaners you use for your pool, only smaller. Sucked it right out. She said she could really feel the pull, all deep up in there. So maybe I'd be home sick in bed too. But why wonder.

They shut the television down late at night and there is not much to see. I do not want to look at the woman who says she's been here since Wednesday, because when I look at the woman from Wednesday all I hear is her voice saying the same thing she always says. She says she's here to be with her husband. I don't know how she thinks she's with him, sitting out here. She didn't ask about me so I didn't tell her about my wife's mother and of course not about my wife. But she did say I was a dear because I got her some bottled water out of the vending machine. She offered me change but I paid myself. People make the biggest deals out of the smallest things. By the looks of her, she is about my father-in-law's age and she dyes her hair, but my wife dyes hers too, and she isn't nearly so old.

My father-in-law is not here right now and I do not think he will be. I have argued about him. I talk to my wife once a day when I call out on the wall phone. I call to tell her that the only news I have is that I have no news and that the doctors still don't know how this could be going on for so long and I am sorry. I say I am sorry because I am and I remember how it was for me afterward, even if I didn't ask my father what it was like for him having to be there and watch. And I ask my wife about my father-in-law. She asks me how I would feel if I were him and I tell her the best I can. I tell her I would feel like a prick who wouldn't know a ticking clock if it bit him on the ass. Those are not my exact words. But I am only answering her question. I think he should be here, and I cannot believe that he's home with my wife while I am here with his. I should not need to tell my wife this but this really is their thing much more than it is mine. Then my wife sounds horrible and tells me that she will talk to me later.

The last time we were on the phone, my wife told me about the arrangements and that she has a suit pressed for me. I haven't talked to her since. My wife told me Friday if it happens tonight, Saturday if it's tomorrow, but if it's the next day everyone waits until Monday. You'd think some things would be above having to wait for Monday. It makes me want to be off somewhere on my own and go to bed without the thought that someone might be tapping me on the shoulder as soon as I fall asleep.

I don't sleep at night, but I have a hard time staying awake during the day. I walk blocks sometimes going around this floor. I go by where I think the operating rooms are and I run my hand along the wall. My right one for a while, then my left the other way, because I like to mix things up and turn around after a few rotations.

The woman from Wednesday is up at night too. There is always the sound of her moving in her chair like she is reaching for something or can't get comfortable. She has all her things in a black cloth bag and she puts her feet up on a beige hassock that is cracked down the middle. Late at night she twists her mouth into an ugly shape and looks up at the ceiling and breathes hard, but only when everyone else is asleep. She has no idea I am looking at her now, and I am sure that if she did she would not say anything. I feel bad for her when she goes to get chips and candy out of the vending machine because she coughs all the time and I wonder if she is sick or just a smoker, and eating out of a vending machine can't help.

I don't eat out of the vending machine, but I have made a game for myself with the digital clock on the other side of the room. Each number is made up of little red bars that are notched on the end to fit into other red bars. The pieces are too small to see from here. Whenever I feel like playing, I look at the wall and try to guess how many bars there are altogether, in all of the digits, in whatever time the clock says. Then I walk across the room and get up close to see if I am right. It is not the greatest game.

The woman from Wednesday sometimes stares at the clock like me, but I think she is doing something different. And I know my wife would want no part of my game, even if she were here. I can tell you that eight past twelve has the most tiny bars in all, twenty to be exact, but my game gets old and it doesn't take long. I can watch the woman from Wednesday in her chair rubbing her eyes, and I move on to that. I feel like I am inside of her head with her and we have an agreement. All I have to do is cough when she turns, and we start from there every time.

SEQUENTIALS

THE WINDOW WELL

When I became single again, and a wife was gone, and the children were gone, and I was gone from myself in many ways, I used to do yard work at a house that had three lawns: a large, sun-coated one in front, a smaller strip of wet-green in the back, and a curving riband on the side, where salamanders slept and could get their backs split open by the rake.

The third lawn had a window well that looked into the house. It was covered by a spider web, which was thick, but you could see through it, just enough. In the well, I saw a snake, probably a black racer. It didn't look like it was moving, but its head and most of its body were off the ground, as if they'd been frozen that way, or the snake was very good at holding still.

I figured it could climb out. I wasn't going to touch it. But I did break the web in a single slice with my rake, as fast a motion as I could make. And then I walked around the corner to the front lawn, to take a break from my work, and I saw a girl who was walking faster than people walk. Walking faster than people run.

She went in one direction, hard, and then another, and when she arrived at each point she arrived in a way that you could not understand. She journeyed and was instantaneous. She was not there, and then she was there. She came, but she also just was.

From farther away she looked tall, very tall, taller than myself, like I was looking up at her even as she stood on the far side of the lawn. Then she was in front of me, and she was lower, at first, as if she was growing up out of the ground, and so close that we were going to collide even though neither of us was moving forward or backward.

I was scared of her, but I wanted to try and help. I wanted to say, as calmly as I could, "What is your name?" but instead I said, "Who are you?"

She didn't stop for breath. The breathing kept going, getting louder and louder. Then it was over, the sound, that is, and she began moving again, from point to point, until she reached the far edge of the lawn, holding a position before starting once more. I put down my rake, with as little movement as possible, and began walking away, quickly, without running, down the path I used as a shortcut that led to the main street.

The rake remained where I left it when I came back the next day. I walked to the ribbon-lawn. The window well was covered once more in a web. I didn't look into the hole. I kept a sawhorse behind the house, and I took some old pieces of plywood from under the deck and nailed them over the openings of the sawhorse.

The sawhorse was bulky now, but I lifted it around the corner, put it over the window well. I had a marker in my pocket, and I wrote "Leave This Here" on the sawhorse's back.

THE REMAINDERS OF LONG DIVISION

The coffee from yesterday warmed up and left in the microwave, the late December sky two hours before the sun comes up outside of smudgy windows. Sitting. The desk. The bed. The bed the desk. It's funny the things we hold onto, physically grip into, because they are the most proximate, and we need them. .

I got an early start today because I want to have a good start to the year. Try to get somewhere. Get what I want. What I need. What I search for. What I used to tell myself at the end of each year might be attained in the next, until I stopped because there comes a point when the pursuer need never remind himself again what is being pursued.

As I was watching a film—*The Twilight Zone* movie, which really isn't very good—I decided to clean out the photos on my phone. Carpet, meet thy broom. Time to get lifted. I don't scroll back through photos, normally. I don't know why I take any. Memory doesn't function that way for me. Like, "Here's a photo, and now a feeling I once had is more real." I hadn't realized how many there were of you. In various stages of undress. I hadn't realized you wore that hat of mine when it got very cold. I hadn't realized I had a photo of that bed soaked through. That blue sheet. Like Linus's blanket gone way, way wrong. The substance of a running joke. Of which no one else could partake. But there it was. I thought, as I looked at some photos of us together, about how your former neighbors, in the town where you grew up, contacted your parents voicing concern. According to you. Because you were posting photos of yourself with someone you said you cared about.

They had no clue I was older. I didn't look it. We didn't look it. Strangers would say nice things when they saw us. "What a happy couple." "You two just go together." But everyone only saw the stage presentation. "I play a part" is how you described it, before I even met you. But if they only knew, right? If they only knew how you lived then, and how you live now. What I embodied. What was there. The shared wavelength, the salubrious presence. What you found wonder in, as I in turn believed in the wonder in you. How much I cared once, too.

One photo stood out in particular. You were working at the dining hall. It was before your shift started. We were sitting together, and you were looking at me with a look that, if I did not know better, if I did not know that no matter how much something looks like something it can always be something else, I would say is love made visual. But I know it wasn't actually that. Still, if I believed such a thing could be conveyed in a look, that photo would have been pretty good proof. Like I said, it can be very strange that we keep the things we keep.

I wonder if someday you'll still have this note, if you ever even see it, if I even ever send it. But yes, strange keepings. Stranger, maybe, what we are left with.

INTO THE PRESENT

I fled the rat's nest I live in earlier tonight because something bad was going to happen if I didn't. I would drink and break my streak of not drinking for fifty days, and I figure, this time, if that starts again, I'll drink until I'm dead.

Went to a nine thirty screening of the 1947 Robert Mitchum film *Out of the Past*. Looked like a crazed homeless person. Didn't have socks on, gym shorts, two weeks' of beard growth. Not that Mitchum would mind, I figured. Grizzled guy. You don't get many chances to see classic film noir in a theatre. Death is on my mind a lot. With death on your mind, that's how you think. "Last chance to dance," so to speak.

I was engaged to someone who was basically Kathie Moffat, the woman who destroys Mitchum in the film. Femme fatale writ overlarge. Some scenes made me jolt, given that it's not easy to encounter someone in real life who resembles Kathie Moffat. And it would be a pretty screwed-up search. Dystopian search. As in, *why on earth are you looking for that?*

I always sit in the same seat—last row of the balcony, dead middle, so everyone else is in front of me. For some reason, that matters to me. Don't like the feeling of having my back exposed to anyone. There was this guy in the front of the balcony, maybe in his early thirties, shaved head. The type of guy you think should have a neck tattoo but he didn't. He was tearing up a plastic container, crunching a can, scrunching plastic bags. Super annoying.

Film ends, lights go on, and everyone in the balcony—about ten people—stands up to take a look at the noise-making prick. The floor around him is covered in ripped-up shit. Blanketed. There's rudeness, and then there's something else going on, and this had to have been the latter.

There was this woman a couple rows in front of me, early forties, very attractive, married—you always note the presence of a ring, when you go through certain things in life—but there by herself. She had gotten a copy of the two-month schedule of films that are in stacks around the theater, and had been circling pictures she'd like to attend before the movie started. I do that. So I thought, you know— maybe. Just maybe. I'm here a lot because I have no life and I have to flee things, and she's here a lot and maybe she's separated, and while I usually go for younger, maybe—maybe—maybe.

We were the last two to leave the balcony, discounting the noise-making guy, who was just sitting there, motionless, head in his hands, oblivious to everything. She started to walk over to him. I thought she was going to ask him if he needed assistance. She got within seven feet, and said, in a fairly sweet voice, "Excuse me, sir, excuse me…but next time you come to the movies, could you please try to keep it down?"

She turned around, reached the top of the stairs, and said, loud enough so anyone up there could hear it, "Asshole."

I don't know. I felt like Mitchum in *Out of the Past* would have read a lot into that, having been through what he went through. Maybe that's why I did. Maybe that's why I thought about walking over to the dude and putting my hand on his shoulder and asking him if he needed anything. Maybe that's why I didn't, and walked out into the night with my head down, more aware than usual of the wind and picking up my pace as I walked into it.

AN INCIDENT IN
CATHEDRAL ROMANCE

The horse descending through the night sky was the first indication to the sentry that a countermove had finally been made. There was also the tip of the blade in the center of the sentry's back. One of the intruders had been bound to gain entry before the others, and that usually happened here up above.

The horse was a new touch. The intruder with the blade gave the sentry a slight push forward in the rampart, where they both stood, atop the cathedral that had once been a cathedral and not a wartime fortress, as it had been for the entirety of the sentry's career. But that was to be expected, in his line of work.

He saw that the horse was not actually moving of its own accord through the night sky—which was a relief—but that it was harnessed in a rig whose ropes and pulleys draped back over the wall meant to keep out invading forces. A chief followed the horse, in a harness of his own. It was actually fairly spectacular, the sentry had to admit. These things always had a lot of pomp and ceremony, but still you appreciated the fresh wrinkle.

The chief was clad in the intruder garb that both sides donned when it was their turn to make an impressive countermove. The brown muslin fabric was form-fitting, and anyone who wore it looked sleek and svelte.

He landed with perfect dignity atop the horse, which had shed its harness and flown down through the final five yards on its own, as if to prove it could. The two pranced back and forth several paces—a familiar gesture—before the chief descended from his mount, walked to the wall that he had just surmounted, and opened the door, so that the rest of the invaders, likewise clothed in muslin, could enter the grounds. "Get in here, you," he might have said, but instead he just waved everyone in.

***

The sentry's part was mostly complete. Again, ceremony. You had to stand on a fair amount of it. He descended from his rampart that had once been a spire, the intruder with the blade now walking at his side, entering one of the rear doors of the fortress that had once been a cathedral.

His own chief was already awake, having expected a counter-move for a long time. "Tell him I will be out presently," the chief told the sentry. The intruder with the knife put the blade back in its scabbard. There was some delay in handing him his cup of broth—as was customary in these matters—but the broth was procured, and the intruder sat down in the chair he usually sat in on such occasions.

The sentry did as he'd been tasked, and then slunk off into a corner of the courtyard. A boy stood in the shadows beneath a dogwood tree, scared and curious. The home chief and his invading counterpart, who had reversed roles so many times, met in front of the latter's horse, which now had a feed bucket strapped to its muzzle. There was much nodding and sighing. The meeting adjourned, and the chief who had gone so long without sleeping waved everyone inside of the fortress that had once been a cathedral. The boy, forcing himself to be brave, followed for the first time. Normally he would go to the pond where the invading chief's horse was watered and throw rocks at frogs that he was never able to hit, save, it seemed, when he was aiming at something else. But maybe that was the trick to getting frogs.

***

The home chief looked wearier than usual. This had been a long time coming. Another cup of broth was procured, but he waved it away, offering it, instead, in the general direction of the group clad in form-fitting muslin. When they passed on the broth, the steaming cup was duly handed to a girl, the boy's age, who made a great show of getting frogs with rocks whenever she had the time to do so, which was not often, as she had more important business to attend to.

The conversations between the two chiefs continued into the morning, and all through the next day, before they concluded in the middle of the night. For these were most delicate negotiations.

Everything, it was decided, was to be done in a more orderly fashion than in times past. If you're going to make a clean break of it, do it right, seemed to be the consensus.

The girl was busier than she had ever been, the boy noticed. He watched her from all angles, on her knees, in the courtyard, with a strip of fabric, rubbing away at the ground. Finally, he summoned the courage to ask her why she was working as she did.

"Don't you know," the girl replied.

"I don't know," he said "I am sorry. Maybe you could tell me all the same? Please?"

"Well, if you must know…"

"Yes, yes."

"If the ground is not smooth, the blood won't be absorbed. When the ground is rough and patchy, it pools there, and who wishes to see that?"

The boy wasn't sure what to say. "So that's what you do?"

"Obviously," the girl replied, continuing to work. "Why? Do you want to do it?"

"No," the boy said.

***

The boy slept in the corner of the courtyard, beneath the dogwood tree, to be near the girl as she worked through the nights. He didn't know if that was okay with her, but she was pretty focused on what she was doing and didn't seem to see him or mind or care.

On the evening the girl finished her work, she waved in the direction of the dogwood tree, so she must have known about his vigil by then, and the boy got up and followed her inside. Nearly everyone was asleep. A few individuals from each side poked at the remains of what had surely been a sumptuous meal. The sentry and the invader who had scabbarded his blade, having long completed his assignment, were debating something—perhaps the finer points of their respective arts—in the corner where the boy usually stood whenever he wished to blend in.

He watched, in the very early morning, as a few people moved about in the half light, careful not to disturb the sleepers. The boy thought that was a nice touch, showing real consideration, even in war, or ceremonial war, or legal war, or traditional war, or ideological war, or manufactured war, or pretend war, or whatever it was. He sat at the girl's side, in the courtyard, not long after dawn, looking up at a man and a woman from the fortress who had lived there a long time, lived with each other a long time.

"Should we do a last kiss?" the woman asked.

"Well, it'd be purely ceremonial," the man answered, like he wished it would have been a different kind of kiss entirely.

The chief of the invaders removed his blade from its scabbard, stepped toward the man and the woman, and then turned and motioned to the invader who had first come up behind the sentry in the rampart, preferring, instead, to watch, as was his right.

"Eh, you have a go," he said.

***

The boy reached for the girl's hand as the blade was drawn.

"You are not to hold my hand now."

"Are you sure?"

"Of course I am sure. You may after he begins. But you must stop when he is finished."

The boy held the girl's hand tight as the first wounds, across both stomachs, clean slices, were made, the blood pouring and spreading in the smooth dirt of the courtyard. The boy expected to see steam rising from it, as when one of the animals was slaughtered in the early morning, but the blood looked cold, like the water from the deepest part of the pond.

Before the second slice was done, which is to say, in mid-slice, the boy had let loose of the girl's hand and got on his knees, working feverishly at the reddening ground with a piece of cloth he had taken from his pocket, as the blood poured from the man and the woman.

"Quickly, help me," he said. "Or they will be no more. They do not need to be no more. There should be proof of what was."

The girl stared hard at him as a third, and concluding, slice was made—a slice that opened, again, man and woman in one motion.

"Why?" the girl asked.

He didn't know what to say. He couldn't believe she had asked. And when you can't believe someone has asked a question, it's impossible to answer them.

With that, the activities concluded. The home chief gifted a formal account of the events to the invading chief several days later when the invaders went back to their own land, where their chief would become the home chief. Such matters are rotational. They flip. People tend to say they even out in the end. The horse over the wall had been a nice touch. That would be hard to top. But someone usually found a way.

**

"And did they invade them?"

Every year, the teacher gave a lesson on the same fable, but he liked to rewrite it in his own hand, and encouraged students to do the same. He felt it helped to cope with life. Not that too many of them had too much to cope with yet. But still, one could learn early.

The conversations generally followed a similar pattern.

A boy would say, "Of course they didn't invade them. That didn't really happen. The invading chief or whatever his name was wouldn't slice open a chick and some guy while everyone just hung out like that."

Then the girls got involved. "Of course it happened. It happened to one of his relatives, didn't it? Stories like that get handed down from generation to generation. Don't you know anything?"

"Well, food for thought," the teacher said, concluding another year, one that had proven harder than the last.

A DEUCE CROSS

My brother Thale was of the opinion that when a preacher was really worked up and preaching hard some lesson about someone else, what he was really doing was preaching something about himself.

He'd tell me stuff like this when it was just me and him out on the back stoop of our small Craftsman house in Covington, sharing a bottle of Cheerwine, our favorite soda, although I never drank it much on my own. I figured he had some expertise. After he turned twenty-one that spring, he started driving around in our mom's '59 Ranch Wagon, hitting up one church service after another, ostensibly making preacher-related notes, which was just something you knew you were supposed to think was impressive.

Thale planned to leave Tennessee in the fall to go to divinity school at Harvard, a concept you couldn't help but laugh over when you studied his peculiarities. Like when I'd hog the bottle of Cheerwine, savoring all of its nasty stickiness, and Thale would say, "Okay, give it over, dickhead." Not really preacher talk. But he didn't say "dickhead" like the rest of us—by which I mean me and my friends in our somewhat less-than-kickass rock and roll band. He said it with class, like you imagine rich people say "chap," "fellow," or "sport." It was all velvety, a neat transformation. You'd try and say it too, Thale's way, but it just wouldn't work, prompting him to call you a dickhead again, and sounding even more rarefied the second time around.

We hung out a lot, me and Thale, given that our dad left when I was seven. He lived out on a ranch in Montana that we never saw. My mom and Thale were close, I guess, but in this weird, unspoken way. They did a lot of talking through looks. Like they were partners in some undertaking you weren't being let in on. My mom was always working a mess of jobs, so Thale kind of got me in a "you do something with him" manner.

Maybe we ought to have been enemies, after a fashion, that final summer. I was all about the Beatles, never mind that John Lennon had shot his mouth off and said the band was bigger than Jesus, and people were pissed where we lived. The really religious people, that is. Amongst whose number you'd think Thale would count, but he had some other business going on that made you wonder what the hell he was doing with the whole divinity school thing.

Thale, you see, was plowing one of the neighbors. That's how Charlie Stickle, the bassist in our band, put it. Everyone knows a kid like Stickle at some point. You figure there's no one else out there like him, and somehow the Stickles of the world stay far enough apart when you're young that you don't get disabused of the notion.

"Man, what your brother must do to that undercarriage. If you know what I mean."

We'd be practicing a new arrangement of something like the Stones' "19th Nervous Breakdown" or the Kinks' "I Need You" in my garage, once the Ranch Wagon had been gotten out of it. Truth be told, I was more interested in seeming like a bona fide front man—and guitar master—in front of Stace Goldchuk, our drummer and a whiz at school. In any class you had with her she'd be the best, and sometimes she'd even correct the teachers, which was near unfathomable.

"He shanghais that undercarriage, I bet."

And then Stickle would kind of squeak hee-haw, hee-haw, a bit like that rich guy in *It's a Wonderful Life*. This would crack up our singer, John Tuskagee, or Tusk as everyone called him, a name he probably got not from his surname but on account of the giant incisor on the right side of his mouth. Meanwhile, Stace would start fiddling with her hi-hat, all of this being beneath her, and I'd try and crack everyone back into line.

"You don't even know what 'shanghaied' means. Just focus on not screwing up the bridge this time."

"Fuck you, Fenner."

Thanks to Stickle, even the teachers at school had stopped calling me by my name, Tim Fenwood.

It was my idea to call our band Toad Rode the Salamander. What can I say. I was listening to what I thought of as super heady stuff at the time. We all flipped when we first heard *Revolver* that summer in 1966; Stickle and I would nearly come to blows arguing about how much better it was or wasn't than *Rubber Soul*.

Our big goal, that summer, was to see the Beatles in Memphis. Not because we knew it was their last tour. No one could have known that. Bands toured—it's what they did. Even a band with a ridiculous name like our band. Didn't matter that our gigs were never more than ten miles from my house. You had to start somewhere.

When we weren't in the garage banging away, we'd be up in my room, listening to old Bukka White records, or Sonny Boy Williamson, with the inevitable British stuff mixed in. My house was like a shrine to shag carpeting. It was so tufty you'd want to mow it. Shag carpeting and stippled glass: highballs, toothbrush holders, cherubs riding on donkeys. Stickle said it looked like frozen jizz.

Sometimes Stace would come to my defense. The mere hope of her doing so made me love her more—not that she knew.

"I think it's nice. Thematic. Consistent. There are worse things than consistent decór. Or maybe you wouldn't understand, Stickle, being a consistent asshole."

It wasn't mean the way she said it. Funny. Funny to all of us. And it'd put Stickle off his stride for a while, which, even as his best friend, made him a lot easier to be around.

So it would go until one of us took his or her turn at the window in my tiny room—the roof of the house sort of folded down over it at an odd angle, so it felt like you were living in some melted-down geometrical form that didn't have a name—and saw Thale in the street below, running sprints. In a sweatshirt and long pants, never mind the insane heat. He ran them until he passed out. Literally until he passed out. He'd puke a lot. Always on the curb, like he was aiming for it. The sight of him would get Stickle going again.

"Looks like your brother has just been in Sally Heise again. Damn. That shit is wrong. Sweet and tasty, I'm sure, but wrong."

Stickle didn't often come down on the side of morality, but when he did, you knew you had a doozy on your hands. Sally Heise was this girl who was always around, it seemed, though she was a number of years ahead of all of us, Thale included, in school and in life. It was hard to think of her as Mrs., but that's what she was now: Mrs. Daniels.

The original Mrs. Daniels had been dead for two years. That was the official version of events, anyway. Mr. Daniels' son, Britt, was a former great friend of Thale's and by then my biggest rival, in music circles and otherwise. Britt liked to run with Stace from time to time. Lunchroom rumors of assorted perversions could leave me shaking in the bathroom, running my face under the tap before the next period began.

The year before, Thale and this other kid, Skip Lorenz, had gone all the way up to New York City, to Shea Stadium, to see the Beatles.

That's how into the Beatles Thale used to be. Britt was supposed to go too, but his band, the Malcs, landed some nice local gigs, for actual money, playing dances called Waltzers—never mind that everything the Malcs played was in 4/4 time. But a road trip was out of the question. The Waltzers were held at the local Knights of Columbus and were popular with the twenty- and thirty-somethings. It was a time of coming and going, when hardly anything felt locked in place. But then Mr. Daniels went off to Vietnam, leaving Britt and Sally and the ever-returning Thale who, despite his fact-finding preacher missions, would come by and do his thing with Britt's stepmom right in Mom #1's bed.

To be fair, Thale was always into Sally. Lots of Cheerwine discussions about her on the back porch, with us staring at the grass and thinking it looked less like real vegetation than the shag carpeting in the house. How my brother was going to marry her and all of this stuff. Moony stuff. I didn't put a lot of stock in it.

I didn't really get Mr. Daniels going away, because he was a local legend. Mr. Daniels, you see, built these mind-blowing dirt bike courses, more artful and sprawling and complex than other dirt bike courses. They were like mazes unto themselves. The one in Covington was this insane tangle of tracks and gullies and side paths. We used to play there before he bought it, back when it was just a forest that we imagined was loads bigger than it really was. Our favorite game involved taking something from a rival camp, something super special—like your baseball card collection, or your pet turtle that lived in a box—and hiding it out in the woods for the other party to find. The rules were you couldn't bury it or put it too far from a path or beyond a certain point. The emphasis was on ingenuity. And, of course, being a good thief.

What you wanted to do, what really earned you bragging rights, was to make off with stuff that wasn't valuable money-wise but had real emotional currency. We'd moved from stupid kid shit like pulling each other's pants down in front of girls to exposing each other in other ways.

One time this kid jumped Stickle from behind, and Stickle's big revenge was to make off with his retainer, an elaborate mouthpiece no one else knew the kid had, stash it in the woods, then howl with laughter when he had to go looking for it with his mom screaming about orthodontic bills for his perpetually fucked-up teeth.

When the woods became a bike track with twisting, snaking lanes, it became known as the Medusa, but every kid called it the Deuce. Fucking legendary. Not Beatles legendary, but maybe about half that.

The same K of C that did those Waltzers the summer before was now doing this battle-of-the-bands thing, with the winner getting two tickets to see the Beatles in Memphis in mid-August. I figured we had as good a chance as anyone, really, except for the Malcs, who were a decent amount better than us. They were older, for starters. Hell, they knew the word "malcontents," or one of them did—their original band name until Britt and his crew chopped it down to the Malcs, the mighty Malcs.

They were an honest-to-goodness power trio, with Britt handling vocals and guitar—he was like Jeff Beck on that thing—and Ted Newstrom, all stolid all the time, playing bass, and this absolute bruiser of a guy, Allie Schmidt, on drums. His kit was huge and even had Ludwig double bass drums, which no one, not even Keith Moon, had at the time.

The Malcs did a lot of rhythm and blues, but they did Beatles covers too, because you had to do Beatles covers. They'd slow them down and make them into what eventually became known as heavy metal. Their takes on "I Feel Fine" and "It Won't Be Long" vibrated the synapses in your head. They were pure power, whereas we had to rely more on finesse: changing time signatures, modulating, and doing these harmony vocals with me and Stace blending our voices together in what I hoped she felt was some extra-musical way.

We'd talk about our repertoire while Thale did his sprints in the street, some weird kind of penance. When my bandmates had gone, Thale and I would go out to the back stoop and I'd ask him if it was worth it, and if it didn't seem pretty at odds with the preacher thing.

"Is what worth it?"

"You know. Shanghaiing that undercarriage." I was trying to be discreet. Sibling fealty and all.

"Are you trying to be a dickhead?"

As though there were more than two syllables there.

"No, I'm not. It's just, you and Britt, you used to be good friends, and I know that's not his mom, or whatever, but his dad is still his dad, so it's not like she's that far from being his mom, in a nuclear sense."

But Thale wouldn't say anything, and I wouldn't add anything, figuring he knew what I was getting at. Better than I did, probably.

***

The battle of the bands unfolded over two gigs, both at the K of C. The first was for regular members and adults over twenty-one who paid a cover charge. The second was for people under twenty-one, with a cheaper cover charge. Teenyboppers mostly. Each band got a shot at two numbers. We did more "mature" stuff at the first one, with this medley of Sonny Boy Williamson's "Fattening Frogs for Snakes" and the Beatles' "No Reply."

The medley went down a storm, and we were elated, especially after an amp crapped out during the Malcs' closing cover of Slim Harpo's "Rainin' In My Heart." The judges—a retired high school science teacher, Mr. Crispin of Crispin's Wholesale Meats, and some lady who gave these presentations at your house for $10 on how best to run your garden—determined that, between the dozen or so bands, Toad Rode the Salamander was the best.

"Fuck yeah, toolbaggers," Stickle announced, bent over in the direction of his crotch as we milled around the Little League field. We were about a mile from the K of C and a few hundred yards from my house, which is where we tended to go at night when there was reason to smoke a joint, which I wouldn't touch, because Stace wouldn't, so it was a matter of watching Stickle and Tusk go to town.

"It was only because of the amp," Stace offered.

"Nah, fuck that. We were good. What do you think, Fenner?"

"Bit of both, probably."

Thale was more specific later that night on the back stoop.

"You're speeding up too much on the bridges," he said, refusing to hand over the Cheerwine.

"How would you know?"

"Because I was there."

"I thought with Britt out of the house you'd be, you know"—for some reason in these instances, I'd try and sound like Stickle—"doing what one cat does to another when you dump them in the same bag."

"What does that mean?"

"Hump. Humping."

"No. I wanted to see you play. Especially now that…"

I knew my brother was worried about going to Harvard. I had this feeling he thought he'd be caught out, revealed as an imposter, a diddler of married women and, what's worse, married women whose husbands built epic dirt bike courses and then went off to fight for their country.

"You don't have to do it, you know."

"The sprinting?"

"No. The cat part."

"Don't say 'hump' again. And stop doing that with your fingers."

"Stickle says, 'and that ain't no donut.'"

"I get it."

We sat there for longer than usual. I liked trying to find the Little Dipper, which for some reason was always a lot less bright than the Big Dipper. I remembered reading that there were some constellations you could only see at certain times of the year, and I was going to ask Thale if that was right—he used to be really into astronomy when we were younger, and even got a telescope one Christmas—but he spoke first.

"He's dead, you know."

I didn't. I figured we were about to get deep, the way Thale liked to do late at night.

"God?"

"No, dickhead." Quieter this time, like the word, and the world, for that matter, had curled up inside itself. "Mr. Daniels. Months ago. Before everything started."

"What? How?"

"Mine. Trip wire."

"A what? What do you mean, a trip wire?" All I could think of was the coat hanger we'd used that time to get into the car when Mom locked the keys inside.

"A trip wire, that's like a bomb."

I knew before he said it, before he took a big breath, then another, that it was a bomb.

He told me where, someplace I'd have to practice to be able to pronounce, which made where matter even less.

"Does—"

"No. Britt doesn't know."

I was trying to decide if Thale was going to cry and if he was, if I should watch him or look away, and all I could manage was "Ah," like grown-ups say on TV. I felt like I was about four, with a painted-on mustache.

I could vouch for Britt not knowing. He was the same as he'd always been, calling me a chickenshit whenever I saw him, but with a big smile on his face.

"How could he even go? Wasn't he too old?"

"I guess he had some special kind of knowledge about forests and deforesting or something like that, on account of—"

"The Deuce."

"Yeah. Things like the Deuce."

I had never put my arm around my brother before, but I did it then. I told him it'd be okay. There was just so much coming off of him, it was like it was his loss. The muscle beneath Thale's shoulder felt as though it was threaded with steel wire. My own felt squishy by comparison. I said the "It'll be all right" line again and the blood went through my face, like when I had to give an answer in class after I hadn't been paying attention and I begged God or whomever not to have the teacher call on me, which she inevitably would. Maybe that was how life worked. It was the first moment I think I ever thought, *Good fuck, I don't know if I'm up for that.*

"I don't see how it could be."

I hadn't expected him to answer. But you figure: in the entire history of friends, brothers, or any two beings who care about each other—husbands, wives, cats in a fucking bag—has anyone ever said things wouldn't be okay? When you learn something big that you know you're going to have to think about later on, because it's never going away, maybe you cut it down, maybe it's too much for then and there, so you leave it. You come back to it because it's coming back for you, but on that first pass you wiggle out a little earlier than you should. I think that's what I was doing. What Thale was doing I couldn't tell, but I think we both knew we needed each other more than ever.

***

It wasn't hard to tell when Britt Daniels learned his father had died. I didn't know who told him, whether it was Sally Heise or my brother. I'd put it that way in my mind but I knew it couldn't have been Thale, in some kind of confessional setting like maybe he'd find up at Harvard. Thale wouldn't have been that easy on himself. He'd have probably been what our mom called "fake careless," meaning you give yourself away when you do something wrong because you want to get caught and have the punishment outpace the crime because you need something to outpace your guilt. But I knew someone had done the telling when I saw Allie Schmidt pummeling Thale outside the Daniels' house.

Allie could whack the hell out of a drum kit—or a lineman, being an all-state tight end on the Covington High team—and as I pulled up on my bike and saw him whacking the hell out of my brother, I could feel my mouth getting all warm, like there was liquid fire in it, until I realized I was biting the inside of my cheek and had to keep spitting blood on the ground. But I knew, too, that Britt's pain, the anger, had to go somewhere, and so for a spell, it went into my brother. Which was how Thale wanted it.

When we learned that the Malcs would be going ahead with round two of the battle of the bands, we were surprised. I didn't want to try and beat them, which now seemed possible, if not probable, given that Britt was bound to be a total mess, and terrified, I supposed, about his future. Stickle heard something about paternal grandparents in Florida, but no one I knew had asked him yet.

"We should really just let them win," Tusk suggested during a hangout session in my room. Thale was sleeping a lot by then; you could only blame it on the beatings he'd been taking.

"Yeah."

Stickle was as terse on the matter as I'd ever heard him. Stace put her hand on his, but she gave me a look as if to say, I hoped, *Don't worry, I'm being a good friend, you and me are something else.* I was a tinder bundle, though. Like I could have gone off and scorched the woods, and I just had to stand there and watch, all unlit.

It was my understanding that each round was won by degrees: that is, if one band—Toad Rode the Salamander, say—was only a little better in the first round, and another band was way better in the second, that band would get the Beatles tickets. I knew we all wanted the Malcs to get them. We were, you might say, hoping to get our collective ass kicked.

It wouldn't have mattered how well we played, to be honest, although we were terrible. There was no touching the Malcs that night. They did a version of "Rainin' In My Heart" that made a bunch of kids grow up awfully quick, if for only three minutes, with Britt screaming the thing so that you could hear, I swear, the blood in the back of his throat. The only time I'd ever heard a singer scream like that was on "Twist and Shout" at the end of *Please Please Me*, but those were happy, carnal screams, and this was a larynx-tearing dispatch from an abyss.

They were the last band to go on that night, and as they finished their concluding number, Stace pressed my hand in hers. I watched as Stickle and Tusk exchanged a glance, like something official had just gone down, but we all knew the bigger thing was happening onstage as Allie Schmidt's crazy double bass drum accents exploded all around us. *Good on them*, I thought. *They won it.*

If only. I figured there'd be this big emotional moment, with Beatles tickets being forked over like some chalice, but Mr. Crispin, of Crispin's Wholesale Meats, just walked to the front of the stage, then back to the side, where a passel of adults his age were gathered in a circle. One of them held up his hands and started touching the tops of each finger on the left with his right index finger, like he was making a number of crucial points. Mr. Crispin, who I imagined smelled of bologna, like he always did, even in church, then came to the microphone with a gravely serious look on his face and said that the Malcs had won that night's contest and now there was a tie with—he had to look at his notes—Toad Rode the Salamander, so there would be a third and deciding gig. I guess they were making good money at these things.

I didn't want to do another one. None of us did.

I walked up to Britt to say as much, conceding, basically, but he had a proposition all ready to go, and he seemed excited enough about it that I felt backing out would have made things even worse for him.

"I say we settle this at the Deuce."

You'd think he lived in a fucking *Gunsmoke* episode.

Stickle wandered over. He'd always fancied himself a liaison because his dad was some sort of sewage company arbitrator. "No. You won. You're better. We're out."

Britt just started talking to me like he didn't even see Stickle, let alone hear him. "Same as when we were kids. Happier times, right?"

He had been there for the retainer incident, with the screaming mom and the crying kid and us hiding in the bushes and all but shrieking with laughter. That flashed through my brain even though, as I looked at Britt, I felt like he wanted to stab me in the throat. We'd almost been friends then.

"Whoever makes off with and hides the thing that means more, we'll call the winner, and fare thee fucking well to simpler times, too."

Now he looked like he was going to start seizing up and just losing his shit.

We argued about this later. Tusk maintained that Britt popped a lot of pills, but I didn't think that was why he wanted to do this throwback thing. I knew whenever I was hurting I tended to look back rather than to what extended out, going forward. Dip into the past and something safer.

I thought maybe it was charitable to go along with Britt this way. Like I was a good person. But maybe I just didn't know what to say.

***

Everything was scheduled for two weeks later. In the meantime, Britt was going to Florida, I suppose to visit with those paternal grandparents. Of course, a lot can happen in a short amount of time. Stickle and I still marveled over how the Beatles went from *Help!*, which we thought was pop shit mostly, to *Rubber Soul* in four months. Who does something like that?

Stace and I started hanging out after band practice, all alone; later, when I'd meet back up with Tusk and Stickle, we'd debate what was going on, if any of it meant anything. My big argument was that she was quieter than before—not more serious, but more grown-up, like she regarded me with deeper consideration when I said something, which caused me to say less because I was worried I'd sound like a tool.

"Something is going to happen, dude," Stickle advised me. "Something in an undercarriage way is going to happen. Especially if you're not a pussy. 'A pussy heart never plowed fair lady,' that's what I always say. Especially with a girl like Stace. You need a big-ass romantic gesture to land a fish like that. Get some blood on the deck, if you know what I mean. And I don't mean in a menstrual way."

We were throwing the baseball around at Stickle's house, and each time he said "undercarriage," he'd fire the ball harder. After the report in my tattered catcher's mitt, I'd turn to Tusk, who would be nodding sagaciously, like the Great Stickle, genius prognosticator, had hit upon his best bit of foretelling to date.

Not long after that, Stickle and Tusk didn't even show up for band practice one day, so Stace and I sat in my room and listened to music alone.

Stace was always smarter than us. That's what we thought, anyway. We struggled to do things like read the poems we were assigned to read out loud in class without sounding like absolute twats, but Stace knew a lot of them without having to look at the page. I'd try and tell myself my appeal to someone like her was that I was a doer, and doers are different from people like Stace, not that she couldn't do lots of stuff, but maybe we could complement each other. Maybe if we staked out enough of a middle ground, I could be something to her like what I wanted her to be for me. Like Thale was, in a way, I guess.

The light was almost brown coming through the shades, this fuzzy calico, and as I sat cross-legged with my back against the wall, Stace moved from one side of the bed to the other, then kind of lay back, so that she was looking at the ceiling and her hair came over the top of my thigh. Her breathing changed; it sounded like she was asleep, but then she mumbled and I heard the name "Thale." When I asked what she was talking about, she mumbled a little more clearly and asked what it had been like, and she seemed to be getting at something big, like this was our crucible moment, so I thought I'd go for it, super go for it as Stickle would say, and open myself up in the way I'd read about but never done because I sucked at that kind of thing. I don't think she wanted me to be an awkward fuck, but in that weird light, with her hair on my thigh, with her head not very far from my, you know, shit just started coming out of me.

"After my dad left," I said, "Thale and my mom seemed to get closer and I was on my own a lot. Or it felt like that, anyway."

"Feeling something doesn't mean it really is a certain way. Do you know what I mean?"

Stace tended to talk carefully when she was being extra nice, like she wanted to make a point but not put it across too hard.

"No, I know. But I was wondering back then if…"

"That if you felt something so much it had to be true."

"Yeah. Exactly. And what I wanted, more than anything, was to be as much a part of everything as they were. Does that make any sense?"

She set her eyes square on mine, and we sat like that for a few seconds. I needed her to speak first. But she knew that.

"So what did you do?"

"It was stupid, really. My dad used to buy my mom Hummel figurines for Christmas. You know, like for a manger. I don't know how many he gave her, but I know she had the Virgin Mary because I found half of Mary in the backyard one day. She'd busted them up with a hammer after my dad left. I found Mary—really pretty much just the head and shoulders—sticking out of the ground, so I dug her up and got some varnish out of the garage and painted her black. I don't know why. And I didn't know what to do with her after that, so I stuck her under my bed. When I got older, Thale lent me a Billie Holiday record and I thought, you know, Billie Holiday was the sound you couldn't hear that lived under the bed, and it had gotten into me after so many years of sleeping on top of it. I wanted to tell Thale but I never could. I thought it'd do something between us. I don't know what. Make me an equal part of something."

For a second I thought she was going to cry, but she didn't. Because she didn't want to embarrass me, it seemed. I didn't want to cry in front of her, but for maybe the first time in my life, I thought it'd be okay to do so in front of someone my age. Instead, I just said I was going to check on Thale. He'd been sleeping a lot lately, which didn't seem like a good thing, and he was leaving soon.

I tiptoed to Thale's door and stood there, listening to him snore. That's really all I wanted to know, just that he was there. When I got back to my room, Stace was sitting on the edge of the bed, her now-naked back facing me. Shoulder blades, a freckle under the right one. A whiter inch or so of skin on the far side of her spine, like your hand could trip up, in a way, as you rubbed from one side to the other. I shut the door as softly as possible, not sure what I was supposed to do. Idiot that I was, I blurted out the first thing that came to mind, which I somehow thought would make a tricky situation more manageable.

"I won't tell anyone."

"Sometimes it's okay to tell."

And then she took my hands and put them on her.

***

We decided to steal Allie Schmidt's bass drums. Or one of them, anyway. It was Stickle's idea.

"Look, we humor Britt, right? His fucking father died and your brother was plowing his father's wife and I mean—let's just humor him. I think he's come undone. Unless he's like some master criminal. A revenge genius. Like he's pretending this is just some battle-of-the-bands shit, but really it's a ruse for something worse, something like what a pirate would do. Piratey shit."

Stickle had a weird love of pirate literature. Sometimes his mother even called him a complicated little pirate.

"They lull you, and that ease sets in," he continued, "and then *boom*, it's up-your-ass time. Anyway—"

"What is wrong with you?"

"I bet it's some reversion shit, like those war vets who curl up in fetal position. You have to be soothing. Anyway, the Schmidts' garage is never locked"—I have no idea how he came by this choice bit of info—"so we go over Friday night, take the fucking drum, put it in a trash bag, leave it out in the open at the Deuce, and then we're good guys who played along, they get to win, and we get to nail some freshman girls next year as a reward."

"I don't think it works that way."

"You don't know that it doesn't."

Fair enough.

Between me, Stickle, and Tusk, we got into the Schmidts' garage easily. Stace, presumably, had better things to do. The only mishap occurred when Tusk disturbed a corn snake who must have thought he had the joint to himself. We huffed the drum over to the Deuce and, with our flashlights, found a nice strip of road, probably a quarter of a mile out into that veritable maze, and plopped the thing down.

I was trying to spend as much time as I could with Thale by then because it wasn't long—just a couple of weeks—before he'd be heading north, although I harbored doubts that he really would. Hopes, maybe. But I also sort of wanted to pop him, the more I turned over in my head what he had done to a kid who, in a sense—and maybe it was the music thing, but it felt like more—I didn't think myself crazily dissimilar from. I mean, if someone told me my dad was dead, it wouldn't have hurt more than not having a dad already did.

The Beatles' Memphis show was on August 19, and Thale was supposed to leave for Harvard a few days after. He wasn't out on the back stoop though, when I got back from the Deuce. He wasn't in his room either, and that was strange, as Thale did most of his wandering during the day. I was damn sure he wasn't over at Britt's place, not after the thrashing Allie had given him. I figured he could have been doing an extended version of his preacher note-gathering deal, like the time he took off for a whole weekend and came back not looking as convinced about something as you thought he wanted to be.

He wasn't there in the morning, either, when Tusk and Stickle showed up on their bikes to ride over with me to the Deuce, to play out our part and make like we were looking for whatever of ours had been hidden there. Nothing seemed to be missing. My guitar and amps were still in the garage. Maybe because we kept it locked? I didn't know. I just wanted everything Britt-wise to be done and to keep everything going with Stace.

There was hardly any activity at the Deuce that morning, just a few stray kids on street bikes doing jumps. We rode around for a while, seeing nothing. The bass drum was where we had left it, but now some blades of grass were starting to grow up around it, like the forest was in the early stages of claiming this bit of percussive equipment. Eventually we sat down under a walnut tree a couple miles out and did what we normally did, which is to say, we started bullshitting each other, Stickle creating yet more terms for parts of the female anatomy and telling us of his recent decision to start calling his dick his coxswain. Tusk and I said we had no clue what that meant, and Stickle said a couple morons like us wouldn't.

"Gotta piss, boys. Back in a bit."

He must have been gone twenty minutes. Tusk and I were arguing about who would've been the better singer, Lennon or McCartney, if they'd had to be solo acts like Elvis, one of the many stupid discussions we had when we got nervous and tried to prove to each other we weren't. That was about when Stickle came running back, looking decidedly un-Stickle-like.

"In the fucking trees."

"What?"

"Hanging from the fucking trees."

"What's hanging from the fucking trees?"

"Like a, I don't know, a big crib, all wallpapered over."

He ran off with an alacrity you didn't associate with Stickle, so we chased after him, and sure enough, hanging from a branch that must have been ten inches in diameter—a sturdy branch—was what looked like a moving box with old wallpaper stuck to it, big enough for a TV and a bass drum, for that matter. It was suspended right in the middle of the air, five yards from any grass or vegetation. The sides were undulating, like something in there was alive.

Tusk, who was bigger and tougher than me and Stickle put together, was the first to speak.

"This isn't good."

"No."

"No."

There was no way to get up there without a ladder—the tree didn't have any low-hanging boughs—so we started back to my house, which felt like a true fucking Lewis and Clark journey but probably took no more than half an hour. We threw open the garage to find Thale standing there, looking all bemused.

"You're here," I stammered. "Thank fuck." I was expecting to find him bound and bloody up there in those trees.

And then it hit me: Stace. Payback. This for that. Like there it was, this concept album sort of thing, with Thale having stolen something from them, and now it was their turn...

I climbed the ladder, picturing Stace all hogtied, some rag stuffed in her mouth, payback far worse than what had been doled out to my brother. Thale, Tusk, and Stickle stood below, waiting to catch the crib-type thing after I cut it down. Not the best plan, probably.

Stickle was the one who screamed. Looking down, all I could see were some corn snakes making a break for it. I took two rungs at a time, afraid of what I might find, but there was just Stickle's bleeding hand where he'd been nipped. No venom, no foul, I guess.

"Fucking snakes," I said. "What is this, a Boy Scout prank? Motherfuck."

Tusk laughed. "What on earth is that?"

Thale, stoic as ever, put his hand on my shoulder. "That's the head and shoulders of the Virgin Mary, Tusk."

Motherfuck, I thought, and I felt my face start to tremble.

Someone knocked the head to the ground. Stickle was looking at me like I had looked at Thale that time when I wondered if he was going to lose it. Thale walked over and kicked what remained of the statue into the brush, and we started home.

Of course, after all of that, I would write a half dozen Stace-based new lyrics for songs I'd been working up the courage to premiere. Suffice it to say, there was a blues phase for a time, lots of Son House imitations about betrayal. A while later, when Britt left for good, Stickle would call what Stace had done a kindness. Of all the fucking people: sex-pest Stickle, a humanitarian.

"But obviously, we need a new drummer."

***

Thale and I sat out on the back stoop listening to *Revolver* on our shitty record player. We kept playing the album through, but it seemed like "For No One" was on a loop. And me being a wide-eyed fifteen-year-old, the line about a love that should have lasted years was like a diamond-tipped drill bit going into me.

"It doesn't mean what you think it means. When people do things that make it look, maybe, like they never cared, or they couldn't care—"

"Doesn't it?" I said.

"Well, it doesn't have to."

For some reason, I didn't blame her. Not even after it had just happened and I felt embarrassed in front of Stickle, though God knows Stickle did things to embarrass himself every day. It was almost like she had helped me help Thale, by being able to better understand him, just before he left, even if that meant Stace and I wouldn't really know each other again.

"It probably helped him more than it hurt me."

"Do you really believe that?" Thale asked, passing me the last of the Cheerwine.

"Not really."

"Good. You don't want to be a dickhead about these things."

Which is to say, as we both knew by then, that dickheadedness was downright complicated.

RED SWEATPANTS

Yoginis and Asher Benjamin, probably not the best of combos for us.

Been doing that a lot, lately. "Us." "We." Almost certainly speaks to how alone you are when you start referring to yourself in the plural in your thoughts, like you have a friend.

Seemed wise at the time. "Been sitting here all day, in this horrible sty of an apartment, come on. We can step away from the desk. Shower. Feel fresh. Air yourself out. Sure, it's dark already, but it'll be good to go out with this yogini."

I date a lot of yoginis, it seems. This yogini had hair three feet long. Mentioned that a few times. Would be easy to spot, anyway. And it'd be a bit like having an architectural tour, too, since I'd be going past a bunch of buildings designed by Asher Benjamin.

He's one of my favorites. Did lots of Federal style buildings in Boston in the eighteenth century. Lots of clean lines. Nothing rococo. A number of his buildings are near an area I thought maybe I'd be all heroic and try to get back, where there's a hospital I ended up in when I couldn't stop coughing up blood because my life had come apart and my wife made like a ghost and left without ever saying why.

You get haunted by something like that. Especially if you don't forget anything. You never have firm ground. Just questions. Questions are quicksand.

I met my wife for the first time at the Mass General Hospital subway stop, down on the street below. I had a joke I used to make back when I made jokes. I told her, on our first phone conversation, that she could spot me by my red sweatpants. She said okay. So the day comes, and I'm standing there and I know it's her, and she's not coming over, but I'm the only other person clearly waiting for another person. Eventually I say hi, and she says that she was looking for someone with red sweatpants, and I make a joke about how it's a little strange to go out with a thirty-something-year-old guy who tells you he's going to be wearing red sweatpants on your first date. That was our first in-person joke. She did yoga, too, but she wasn't a yogini. I think that's like attaining Yoda-type yoga-person status. I don't care for yoga.

After she was gone, I didn't want to lose what those Asher Benjamin buildings meant to me, with the orderliness of their designs. Even if they were clustered around where we first met. Living like I was in *La Boheme* was bad enough, in a shithole apartment packed with junk from what feels like a previous life.

I remember exactly where I was standing that day I ought to have had my red sweatpants on, not fifty paces from Longfellow Bridge, which goes over the Charles River, the skyline to your left, Charlestown to your right. Everyone else calls it the Salt-and-Pepper Bridge because there are these enormous shaker shapes atop it.

They're a hundred feet above the water. You can die from there, if you jump. It's a decent sign you're close to done, and being okay with it, when you measure your life in how much of something it would take to kill you. Not the best metrics. Mine used to be rosier. Like when I ran into the building president back before I met the girl who wished to date a man with red sweatpants, and he said, "Your air conditioner is in the window over the fire escape. Will you be able to get out if there's a fire?" And I told him, "I'll probably be able to kick it out and get on the fire escape that way, but even if I can't, I can just launch myself out one of the other windows because it's only the third floor and I'll probably survive. If I was up on the fourth, I'd pick up about eighty miles per hour more velocity, and that would finish me."

He said he was glad I had a plan.

I have a friend who tries to keep me alive. He lives out of state. We've seen each other once in fifteen years. His wife thinks that's odd. He tells me she believes we should be going out and watching football games and being "besties." He's also quick to tell me that is her word, not his.

A lot of the time my friend tries to convince me I'm not already dead. Because I usually think I am. I think it's possible that when you die, you're not officially told. Why do you have to be officially told? So you can be dead and in hell, where things happen that couldn't happen out in the normal non-hell world, but you wouldn't know it—you'd just think you were alive as usual.

But he just tells me I'm not dead. That's what I heard on my cellphone as I looked at those shaker-type structures on the Longfellow when I went out to meet the yogini with the three-feet-long hair.

I had just passed the hospital subway stop on the mainland. Seeing it is a nightmare. I replay the sweatpants joke, I think about the color red, I think about the blood I was spitting up that caused me to go to the hospital thirty yards down the road, near the first Asher Benjamin building I was trying to enjoy again before that stretch of Boston became like all of the other stretches, another haunted road of a haunted town.

I'm on the cell phone with my friend, talking about hell, saying how I'm fucked for work, and how I'm working myself to death, or a second death, if the whole hell thing is true, but all I can do is work, lose myself in it, because I can't face anything else.

And then she's coming toward me. I think. Her. My wife. Or the person who had been my wife. Not the yogini. On the Longfellow Bridge where the salt-and-pepper shakers are a hundred feet above the Charles. I've not seen her since my life came apart and death became a real comfort, a real option. Because if you're in hell, think about it: Maybe you can die again to get free. Maybe that's what springs you. It can't just drop you back there, right? You must get redistributed. That's how you beat the system.

I'm six one. So's she. Few women are as tall as me. Now, to get to where the yogini wants to meet, I have to walk past where this person I loved works. I'm not over there much, because that's the other side of the river, and I don't care for the other side of the river. But it's not her closest subway stop, the hospital stop, which she might be heading toward now, it bothers her so bloody little. Or this is in my head. But I'm thinking, "This is her. Should we say something? We have to say something." It's cold, and she has a hood on. But tall, super thin, coming from the right direction. Me, I look different too. Bearded, long hair. Never used to have long hair. Never used to brainstorm plans to leave hell. Worried about ending up there, once.

I keep talking to my friend on the phone. Normal. But I change directions. I'm going to see who this. If only, if it turns out to be her, to ask why, why did she do this to us, to me? Who does it to anyone? I wasn't going to ask that question. Just the big one. She wouldn't answer. Because there is no answer. People don't realize that things can get so fucked that nothing can explain them away. For instance, if she said, "I went back to my first husband—I always loved him more, you were this artist guy I got caught up with and entered into a marriage with when I shouldn't have." Well, that doesn't explain why there was this need to take my cheap computer from me, or a video game console which held about as much appeal to someone like her as her yoga mat did for me. Fucking yoga.

I'm talking work-biz speak to my friend on the phone as I reverse field. And she, well, she had heard it a million times. Or enough. Something about this editor, that book, that writer. And she starts looking back. This person. Quickly. Then she starts hauling ass. Not running, but as close to running as you can get without running.

I'm thinking, "Wow, she's fleeing from us. Me. This is flight. It's not someone who has to get home fast to take a piss or start dinner." But I'm also thinking, "Dude, you're a guy who thinks you're in hell. We've been through a lot. Maybe someone else wouldn't think twice about this, maybe she's not going that fast at all."

I didn't used to say "dude." It's new. Like her wearing earrings that one and only time we saw each other after she left. For eight hours. She wanted to be held, touched, kissed. I was so happy to see her. Later that night, she said in an email I made her miss yoga, and I hated yoga even more because that was the first time I had spoken to my wife in more than a month. But the earrings. She never used to wear them. I knew I was in even bigger trouble when I saw them. That I was collateral damage in a way, that she was starting to think her life had always been messed up, and she had no identity, and now it was girl power time, or something like that, like when she told me—that day we saw each other, just the one, after she had left—that until two weeks before, she didn't even know what was her favorite kind of pizza. But it was cheese. She said it so dramatically. And I remember thinking, "That's a pretty boring fucking discovery. You'd think if you took you almost forty years to figure out your favorite kind of pizza, it'd be pineapple crossed with African fish parts or something suitably diversified and rare. But cheese?"

I can feel my blood pressure going up as I walk at this person's heel. On one of the days when I was spitting up a lot of blood, I had gone to a pharmacy at one of those Minute Clinics and they wanted to ambulance me—what a verb—to the hospital. But I was thinking, fuck no, this could be passage out of hell. You don't say that to the pharmacy doctor person, though. But my blood pressure was so high she wouldn't tell me what it was. Alarming, I guess. But I could kind of feel that it probably was alarming. You can actually feel it moving through you that way, I think, your blood and all.

I can see the subway station in view as I beat pavement, trying to keep up with this person who might have once been my wife. Can you imagine if—the day you met someone you loved, who you thought you'd always be with—some angel or demon came up to you, sort of hovering in the air. And it hit pause on everything, so that person you're going to love stopped moving, traffic stopped moving, everything but this hovering—I kind of picture him almost vibrating—and then the demon or angel said to you, "So this is the first time you're seeing the love of your life. Kudos on the red sweat-pants joke. But, in a few years, you're going to see her here on this very spot, more or less, for the last time, and it's going to be dead dark, and there won't be red sweatpants, but as a result of everything that went down with her you worked yourself to death, basically, and there's blood and it comes out of somewhere in your chest. And there's what may or may not have been a stroke, too. So, what do you think? Really weird, right? Same fucking spot, or pretty close."

Un-pause.

The two of us come to a traffic island at the end of the bridge. My friend who tries to convince me I'm not dead and in hell isn't on the phone anymore. We lost the signal. That reminds me of some joke in an old Boris Karloff and Bela Lugosi film where one of them says, after the power goes out or something, "Even the phone is dead."

The woman on the island looks at me, furtively, a few quick times, as we wait for the light to change. I am staring hard. In fact, I feel like that red and orange-faced guy with the double-sided lightsaber in one of those awful Star Wars prequels, that Darth guy. Not Vader.

Maul. Darth Maul. Like when he was fighting Obi-Wan Kenobi and this transparent force field thing separates them for a minute and he's staring, hard, through it, waiting for it to go away. And I'm leaning. I'm looking so hard I'm leaning, because I want to ask my question that is not going to get an answer, a question for which there could be no satisfying answer, which is to say, one that provides an explanation for everything. I just want to ask my "Why."

But I know I'm a wreck. And my thought process goes something like, "Maybe this is some random woman. Maybe she thinks we're following her. Don't cause a scene. And we don't see well in the dark. It's so dark. Is November in Boston always this dark? Let's try and have her say something. Or make totally sure it's her. Can we get creative?"

So that's what I try to do, for the first time. When the light changes, she goes through the crosswalk. There are several of them. They sort of make a half circle from the bottom of the bridge and then bring you around to the subway station where the red sweatpants joke played out. I stay put, like I'm not going where I think she's going. But I am. She takes the crosswalks, and I put myself in the traffic. Stop the cars, risk getting run down, could well be on my way out of hell, if that redistribution theory is correct. And so I come to stand on the very spot we first met, having beaten her, as-the-crow-flies style, to the front of that subway station.

She's across the street. She doesn't want to cross now, because there I am. Or is this simply a woman who is trying to remember if she should pick up anything in the CVS behind her? But she's staring at me from the other side of the road. Cars are racing past, and you have to look over them and in between them to see someone by the pharmacy, or someone in front of the subway stop, but I'm pretty sure she's seeing me and I'm seeing her. Then she turns and heads into Beacon Hill. I think I see her stop and take a look back, so I wave.

That seems like a good idea. And then I figure it's time to go back over the bridge to deal with this yogini and her hair, for our date, but it takes me about twenty second to think, fuck that, ask your question you can't get an answer to, man.

So I head into Beacon Hill. I go past another Asher Benjamin building. I bought an etching of this one for $75. I don't have that kind of money. But when you know you're going soon, you don't care as much. You can't take it with you, as they say, but maybe you just kind of want to hang out with it for a bit. Couldn't bring myself to look at it in my sty, though. I lost it, actually, amidst piles of crap from a former life.

I catch up with the woman again after passing Asher Benjamin's latest Federalist design. I had to run to overcome that head start she had. She turns into a warren of streets. Beacon Hill, in the warren of streets part, is right out of Victorian London. If the Ripper went racing past, he'd not seem incongruous, you'd just think, shit, there goes the Ripper, I wonder what body part he cut off tonight, or if Holmes and Watson emerged from an alley you'd count yourself fortunate that you got to see them at work.

I know my pressure is like 220/130 by now. I'm terrified. I don't want it to be her anymore, because I don't want further evidence that I might be dead and in hell, because this does seem like how hell would go, and now I simply want to see a woman, a stranger I've never met, not someone I loved who became a stranger, go into an apartment building she's lived in for a long time. Maybe a woman I've scared, who thinks some stranger reversed course on the Longfellow Bridge to follow her. Maybe someone who has taken no notice of me at all.

I go up the hill. The woman is standing on a corner. There is fog. There is actual fog. But it's low fog, so it's down around your feet, no higher than your knees. And it's so dark. There is no one out. Save for the parked cars, it might as well be 1873. It looks like I figure 1873 would look. We are ten feet apart. I stop. I lean again, I stare. She has her phone in her hand. That's not very 1873. It makes me think of a cocked gun. Like she's put a number into it and is waiting to hit send and launch some signal of sorts. But I just want to ask my question. And I'm so scared.

I pull out my phone. I'm just a guy making a call. That happens. You can stare hard at someone you're alone with on some scary-ass street, wondering if it's the person you once gave your life to, and then make a call. So I do. With an ulterior motive, too, a utilitarian motive, deploying a technique that I hope will resolve this situation, almost by accident, but one that is actually staged and clever.

That's when I hear the sirens. They're like an alarm clock. And I start walking again. Out of that low-lying fog, without looking back. Quickly. To be reabsorbed, such as I can be reabsorbed, on the busier main street, not sure what happened, who she had summoned, and forgetting that the hospital wasn't a quarter of a mile away, and ambulances were coming in with the dead and near dying.

I call the yogini as I walk past the hospital. I cannot do it, I say. I cannot make our date. Sorry. I hang up. She is better off.

I can't look at the Asher Benjamin buildings as I venture back to the sty. You think about points of no return. Something like that usually sounds so grim, but when you go to a really bad place, you can tell how bad it is by how well you're able to recognize that a point of no return can be good. You reach a point in your career where you're so successful you could never return to having some lesser position. Something like that. Or you can get so over something that there's no point of return to that place of pain you were once in. Maybe that little hovering devil dude had reached a point of no return of his own that day he turned up, hit pause, and couldn't help himself from sharing something with you that he wasn't supposed to, and then he could never go back to from where he came, and was redistributed himself. Or maybe you come back inside your apartment, start looking for an etching that you couldn't afford that you know you won't find, until you just say, fuck it, and check your answering machine to hear your own voice, sounding dead terrified but perfectly clear enough, saying the word "why" more times than you can handle as you slip into your sweatpants—green—for the remainder of the evening.

THE EFFECT OF GRAVITY
UPON THE TUB

Lorcan, for once, spoke first.

"You heard it too, then? The shower is on. He wasn't hit hard enough."

Despite the circumstances, he worried that perhaps he had made his partner apoplectic. It was not difficult to do so.

"Of course I heard it too, Lorcan. If we are both standing here, having come from different portions of our temporary home—the proof of that visible even now, as I stand here clutching the aforesaid volume of Bryon I set off to find, and you the flashlight from down in the kitchen—it follows that we both heard the sound of what I presume was a man falling to the ground, each on our own, with the shower still running, and came to be standing here on this landing, second floor, together. That is what we poet philosophers call a syllogism. *He said affectionately.* See? That is my new thing in my latest wellspring of verse. I shift narrative perspective. First person to third, just like that, even though it's the same narrator. Brilliant, yes?"

Lorcan, as ever, felt himself approaching new lands, despite having known Padraig for many years in a career in what the latter termed "artful crimes."

"One of us should go in there. I'll flip you for it."

"Nay, my friend, nay. I like going in. Kindly equip me with the blade."

Lorcan handed Padraig the knife from a makeshift leather compartment sewn to his belt, and watched as Padraig brought the blade close to his lips, as was his habit, and ventured into the bathroom.

Lorcan waited anxiously for a few seconds, before his partner reemerged.

"Well?"

"He's passed out. Jaw looks pretty well sunk in. That soldering job on the foot of the aptly named claw-foot tub did not come off as well as I had hoped. Maybe you were right—I should have let Mrs. Rosenlea tend to it. Her overconfidence in the matter bugged me, though. Charming colloquialism. Bugged. Much like the rooms we have been in many times."

"Maybe we should pack and flee."

"Sure. But we have time for a meeting, at least, first. To figure out next moves. His jaw was all squishy. There were teeth. For Hoovering. We have time. Maybe best to leave Mrs. Rosenlea out of this, though, for the time being. The clean-up job can wait."

"I'm not sure I trust her."

"Aye."

***

The evening had begun typically enough.

"I am desirous of getting live-wired, Lorcan," Padraig had said. "On this latest case of Miller High Lifes, the self-professed Champagne of Beers. I guess that's good? Better than the beer of Champagne? Actually, I reason that would be quite tasty. Although, technically, they call a thirty-pack a cube, not a case. And so I shall get live-wired on this cube of beery Champagne."

This was a standard pronouncement in the house in the small coastal town where the two had come to dwell for a time, a recent spate of jobs having been successfully completed, it seemed, and after which they had been instructed, by their last shadowy employer, to make their way toward the sea.

"Alcohol is a barbiturate. Slows you down. Doesn't speed you up."

"As you have said many a time, Lorcan. But I find it is not the case with me. Now: shall we get live-wired, or shall we get live-wired?"

"You know we have a guest coming."

"A mere formality."

But Lorcan knew that mere formalities were rare in their line of work. He had been the first to notice the flashing ray of light from the outside, which seemed to gather intensity with the aid of its blackened backdrop, an expanse of street on which all activity seemed to stop once the sun went down.

"There it is again."

"There what is again?"

"The light."

"I'm telling you. It's Mrs. Rosenlea's husband in their charming cottage across the street. With his telescope. He's an astronomer. The reflection of mere moonlight in the Fresnel lens. Mini Fresnel lens. Had us a nice chat the other night. 'O Mr. Padraig, how are you, sir? Penned any new verse lately, that will doubtless last as the very best verse does?' 'Why yes, I have, Mr. Rosenlea. And my compliments, sir: your wife does a splendid job cleaning our temporary domicile. Thank you for recommending her that first day I had the pleasure of making your acquaintance.' *He said suavely.* See how I did that? My first to third person shift again. Subtle. Dark bird in the night."

"I don't think it's him. Mr. Rosenlea, that is. Go to the window. See? It goes off by the time you get to the blinds."

"Fancy. I think I am going to get live-wired all the same."

Most evenings Padraig would sit at the piano he could not play, occasionally picking away at the keys, informing his partner that he had resolved to master avant-garde jazz—"I shall endeavor to become the Irish Cecil Taylor"—before settling in with a book, generally a pricey first edition that he had stolen for himself during one of their various jobs arranged by the man they only ever called Kalish, although that was likely not his actual name.

In the morning, Lorcan would pull his friend out from under the piano, where he normally decamped—a result, in part, of the live-wiring—and they would try to get through another day, despite the boredom, which usually meant exploring the caves along the shore, where Padraig gathered driftwood and Lorcan, as usual, fretted that something must be amiss, as life was rarely, if ever, this placid.

"Busman's holiday, mate," Padraig offered. "The artistic criminal variety."

But it was not easy to put Lorcan at his ease in such matters.

The last job—involving several forged Winslow Homer canvases, reputedly discovered in a shack in Maine where Lorcan had once summered, and various art authenticators on the take—had wrapped up handsomely. Digital communications were not trusted in such matters, and so a man named Dange—a Kalish associate whom Padraig and Lorcan had never met before—was coming to pay a visit and ascertain where the canvases were at the moment.

"As I said, Lorc, a mere formality. That is funny, though. Every time you walk to the window, there it is."

"Probably just some kids. Right?" Lorcan's voice was shaky.

"Shut the lights out completely."

Lorcan killed the lights and watched, in the low-level darkness, for it was just past dusk, as his partner slowly made his way out of the room and headed upstairs, where a large bay window afforded a better view of the street.

"Well?"

"Well what?"

"What did you learn?"

"That the first edition of Shelley's *Queen Mab*, which I stole from that antiquarian book fair in Old Chi back last spring, was indeed where I left it after last night's libation spree and the impromptu game of hide and seek, with veiled literary references as clues, that I also invented last night and wished to play and had to play on my own. Given your tendency to pout."

"Why did you do that? It was supposed to be part of the package. They always notice the one thing that goes missing. Especially when it's one of the more valuable things."

"Relax, sir, I stole this one fair and square. A replacement volume made it into that package of yours, which we dutifully shipped. We are golden, as they say."

They sat in the darkness, listening to each faint stirring the other made. Lorcan was not accustomed to sensing nervousness in his friend, but the occasions on which he did had preceded some of the darker moments of his life. Few men, if any, were less readily fazed than Padraig.

"Where are you going, P?"

"I'm going to the window. An additional look. Quiet it down for a minute." Rarely did Padraig advise quiet.

"There it is again. They can't possibly see us. What gives?"

"This is well done, Lorcan. Artful, even. And low budget, too. Like someone on the inside is tipping off someone on the out. Are you tipping someone off, Lorcan?"

"I am not, Padraig."

"And nor am I, Lorcan."

"Still want to get live-wired?" Lorcan managed, trying to sound hopeful, but convincing neither of them. "Slightly live-wired might

work. Not too much dulling of the faculties, though. All things considered." His head turned, and his eyes scanned in the direction of the
street from whose other side light occasionally flashed in a weak beam
that nonetheless reflected off the far wall of their temporary home.

Silence was rarely encouraging with Padraig, but a full minute
must have passed before the man who fancied himself a master Irish
poet, and artful criminal, answered his companion.

"Maybe best not tonight, L. How about we light a candle and
wait for our guest. And let's just keep away from the window."

***

The expectant knock came right on time—to the second, Lorcan noted, as he looked down at his watch—but the man on the
other side of the door, when Padraig opened it, was not the expected
Dange, but rather the very unexpected figure of Erskine, Kalish's
chief competitor, whom the pair had met on several occasions.

Lorcan immediately reached to his pocket for whatever manner
of weapon might have been resting there, but Padraig put his arm
atop his friend's, while simultaneously greeting their visitor.

"Odd."

"What?" Erksine answered.

"Odd. As you must well know. You are not equipped with a
flashlight, are you?"

"More like an offer. Can I come in?"

"Don't steal anything."

Whereas Dange was, by all reports, tall and muscular—he'd been
a champion sprinter in Derry—Erskine was anything but. A lumpy,
furrowed creature, he was renowned for being able to fillet a man in
the space of a minute. Lorcan noted how Erskine looked more rum-
pled than usual, as though he had come from a rugby scrum. There

was sweat beading along the side of his head, making his ginger hair glisten in the candlelight, which Padraig now extinguished, flipping on the main ceiling lamp instead.

"Can of the High Life? Should you wish to get high-wired."

"I don't drink."

"Yes. I remember now. As I said. Odd. What's that on your hand there?"

"Mud. Had a bit of a tumble."

"Ah. These things happen."

"Yes."

"Lorcan: let us repair to what we now term the meeting room upstairs—merely an unused guest room, strictly speaking—where we keep the soft drinks and assorted goodies in the mini fridge, and find some refreshment for our guest. Yes? Sound good, everyone? That way you can think of what you'd like to say to us, and we can try to determine why you are really here, something which would doubt-less be abetted by the two of us pooling our intellects in private. You understand how these things work."

"Quite."

Lorcan, to the consternation of Mrs. Rosenlea, had drilled a hole in the floor of the guest bedroom, which was directly overhead what Padraig called the backup meeting room, otherwise known as the kitchen, where Erskine now sat.

"What's he doing?"

"Nothing. Just sitting there."

"He's not using his phone?"

"No. Look, P…"

"I don't know. I suppose we're expected to run him through? That would be company policy here? Maybe we could do something with those caves of yours. Tides and all. People must get caught in there from time to time, yes? We could use my subtle incision technique—the one where it's more about nicks and bleeding out than a single mortal blow. Then we pop him in a cave and late nature do her thing. Then again…"

"No, Padraig."

"We could listen. Maybe he has something for us. Something even more…artful. And lucrative, perhaps. You like that part."

"But it could be something else. We've been out of it for a bit. Maybe it's a test?"

The duo made their way back downstairs with a variety pack of sodas—purchased by the estimable Mrs. Rosenlea during one of her runs to the Stop and Shop—and a bag of sour cream potato chips. Padraig sat at the piano bench and retrieved his copy of the Shelley volume from the floor, while Lorcan asked to what they owed this surprise visit, not adding that it came exactly at the time when another man had been expected to have arrived.

The response was troubling. There had been some shakeups during the duo's respite, apparently. INTERPOL had seized onto the English arm of Kalish's operation, and crates of ancient Corinthian coins, looted from various Greek museums, had been discovered at a warehouse in Leeds, along with several Beatles master tapes that had gone missing from Abbey Road Studios in London, and which were then used to press up some second-generation reels that were auctioned for a fortune in Tokyo.

"So I'm offering you an opportunity. Same capacity with me as you had with Kalish. But a higher percentage. Twenty percent higher. Now, I know, in these matters, there's a sense of some risk involved. Shifting allegiances and all."

"Well, there was Black Tad," Padraig offered. "You did fillet him, essentially. As we all know. Ribbons. Ribbons turned into smaller ribbons. No one wants that." Padraig rubbed his forearm. "We're firmly anti-ribbons."

"Yes. There was certainly Black Tad." Erskine appeared almost wistful. Lorcan felt like he might throw up. "I know it's a lot to consider. A step up in the world always is. Ideally, we'd start with those paintings. The latest batch. Word travels, of course. If not exactly the specifics of the location. Obviously, I've come a long way, boys. One only goes a long way when one is serious about the best."

"By best do you mean most artful? *He said incredulously.* That's my subtle thing I'm doing now, first to third person shift. Still working it out."

"I think he means most profitable, Pad."

"As your friend says."

Padraig got up from his piano bench and walked to the window. He pulled back the blind and looked down the darkened expanse of the street where no one seemed to venture after the sun went down. There was no ray of light, this time, only the flickering of a few fireflies who, to Padraig's surprise, had managed to live on into autumn.

"We'd have to think about it, of course."

"That's fine. I have until tomorrow. I am expected in New York. Making a quick tour of the Northeast corridor, as it were. If you might be able to put me up for the evening…"

"Fine. Take the room at the far left upstairs."

"And can I trouble you for the use of your shower? One tends to get somewhat grimy in one's travels, as you can surely attest."

"It's at the top of the stairs."

"Cheers, boys."

***

"How can you be reading right now?"

"I'm listening, Lorc, always listening. But you're not saying anything. Besides, one might say that the true poet both emotes and listens simultaneously, just as the true lover reaches around to work the frontispiece of his companion—if she is female—so that they too may emote, so to speak, simultaneously. One must joke. Or stress can drive one mad."

"Yes."

They sat in the candlelight. Padraig had donned his pea coat and scally cap, which suggested an air of flight. The cool whiteness of his face aside, Lorcan could barely make out his partner in the glowering darkness which seemed to bite at the edges of the room. The man they had knocked unconscious—courtesy of a blow from Padraig with an enormous cutting board that had recently held a cooling frozen pizza—had been deposited in the upstairs bathroom, in the claw-footed tub, after much pulling and lugging between the two friends.

"We could just take Mrs. Rosenlea up on her offer to borrow her car, stick him in the back while he's still out—you don't even need to cut him down to anything—and leave him in one of the caves."

"Have you checked the tide clock? He might just walk out. Un-drowned. There it is again, by the way. The light. See it?"

"I do. Step away from the window, Padraig."

Padraig did, and walked back to the other side of the room, where the piano was. He stood in front of the soundboard and pulled aside the blind on a second window.

"Two lights now. One on each side."

"Could be kids. It's not kids, is it, P?"

Normally, on those rare instances where Lorcan anticipated silence from his friend in response to a question, he was proven wrong, and this case was no different. It was always reassuring to hear Padraig's voice whenever Lorcan expected silence.

"Right. Meeting adjourned, mate. Let us reconvene upstairs. To the body, then."

***

They stood on the landing, listening to the water rush out of the showerhead, which Padraig preferred to use for his washing up.

"I thought you shut that off after you rinsed your hands."

"I must have forgotten."

"It could have brought him to."

"He was pretty busted up. Anyway, he'd be out here now, wouldn't he?"

Lorcan became ever more uneasy when his friend found occasion to be terse in his manner of speaking. Seldom did Padraig view any situation as one necessitating economy of language, but there was no debating that this was a decidedly new situation for them both.

"Right. I'll go back in. Check on his status. Blade me. That means hand me the knife. If I require assistance, I'll let loose my patented banshee cry."

Padraig emerged back on the landing almost as quickly as he had entered the bathroom, after shutting off the water.

"Come on."

"What?"

"Come on. Quickly now. Faster than that. Faster."

Lorcan felt himself nearly pulled down the stairs and out into the night, his friend clasping him by the wrist. He stood shivering in front of Mrs. Rosenlea's Subaru as Padraig attempted to break the lock.

"Shouldn't we just ask?"

"She's not here, is she? And we no longer have cell phones. For the time being. Obviously."

Eventually, Padraig got the door open by kicking through the window. He attempted to hot wire the car, but it wouldn't start.

"Look under the hood, Lorc."

"There's no engine."

"This is less than ideal."

They both turned around several times in the driveway, looking for where the lights might have come from.

"What was in there? Why are we out here?"

"I believe maybe we've erred. In a not insubstantial way. I think it might have been Kalish. I think he may be Kalish. I think they're maybe both Kalish."

"That's impossible. Don't do the whole 'I'm an especially imaginative brilliant Irish poet prone to being very imaginative' thing, *he said pleadingly.*"

"Nice shift to the third person, even in a moment of admitted crisis. Unnatural order has become general in our coastal hamlet, L."

"This time we look together. Got your blade?"

"Bladed," Padraig said, although he knew they'd likely have little need for weapons when they returned to the bathroom. "And you?"

Lorcan patted his jacket pocket, where he always kept his spare knife.

They walked the twenty yards back to their temporary domicile and passed through the open door that Lorcan had neglected to close in their haste.

"Ready?"

"In we go, then."

The bathroom, save for two details, was in immaculate condition. Discounting the two friends, it was also void of another complete human entity. They immediately saw—as Padraig had previously—that the claw foot of the tub had snapped off, and the front basin portion was resting flat on the floor.

"Maybe it snapped and the fall jarred him and brought him to?" Lorcan half wondered aloud, half asked his friend. He wouldn't have asked the question if any other person, living or dead, was present, but there was no one on the floor, in the tub, or on the floor of the tub. The window was closed, but not all the way, like it had recently been opened and hastily, incompletely shut.

But it was not the state of the window, telltale though it was, that gave the most pause—or that Padraig now wanted Lorcan to see for himself, lest he doubt the telling of the tale later, on the lam—so much as the object in the center of the floor.

"Hmmm. It's certainly fresh. Not a relic."

"Jesus Christ. That's a…"

"Indeed. That is a hand," Padraig concluded, as anyone possessing eyes would have had to.

"They say Kalish has a thing for cutting off hands. When someone has transgressed. Was that him? He had that sack with him."

"There was no sack. Actually, wait. Yeah. There was. Little knapsack. Discreet. Someone else's hand in it, probably."

They stood for a full minute wondering what to do.

More than anything, there was one thing Lorcan did not wish to see, which confirmed that he was probably about to start seeing it.

"There it is. The light. They have one on us up here now too."

"Yes. Did you check the tide clock while we were downstairs?"

"It's not high tide until just after dawn. There would be room in the cave. We'd probably not drown."

"Lucky. They must be getting more people. Stay low to the ground. And stay right behind me, Lorc. *He said with alacrity.*"

"Move, Padraig."

"I'm moving, Lorcan, we're moving, here we go, moving, shhhh, quiet now, moving…you're dropping the hand, dropping the hand, dropping the bloody hand from your hands having picked it up, okay, soft thud on the floor, better it than you or I…only run if I say run, ssshhh, or there are shots, though they probably wouldn't risk that …down the stairs…we're ready to open the door…deep breath, come on, deep breath for me…moving now, quiet, quiet, *quiet for heaven's sake he said breathlessly…run, run.*"

JUNCTION REGALE

It's not really killing yourself in the strict killing-yourself fashion if you only commit to the thought of killing yourself, I have decided in what has become a fantastic day of decisions and medicine-taking.

The train stops at the junction in Chichester and you have to sit for hours before it's ready to leave again, waiting on a dinner car, apparently traveling on its own, to arrive from Slough or Aldershot or Woking—I never seem to remember where.

It was in the middle of my roamings today, in the middle of a crosswalk, before leaving one place I cannot stand for a journey to one where I would rather never be, that I closed my eyes and so skillfully settled upon my decision—post-medicine—which I am now seconding as quite right, in my thoughts, in principle, with the able counsel of brother Gabriel. My cause has not been helped by my most constant dose yet of court proceedings on television—five sustained days, counting videotaped reruns of trials past, at night, when the informercials come on, and the thoughts that refuse to stop sounding in my mind, and my mother too, in whose direction I am again waiting to be traveling, my ever-living mother in the middle of what might as well be an ocean. And, of course, the death; the soiled-bandage smelling rot that would leave me cold were it not for my budget-priced collection of requiems on the Naxos label, my very favorite record label, such important historical recordings and all quite cheap.

I might add, first, that you may do as I do, though situations can of course be tricky and variable, quite naturally. So be prudent. And second, that I am, shall we say, intoning the word *malfeasance* throughout this day of mine, though of course one has to rather whistle it down if a train must be boarded. We have a full house today, the conductor will say, though let it be known that the misrepresentation of a domicile for a machine of travel is not my error. In addition to pondering what happened the last time at the junction in Chichester—so drastically different—I did indeed look up the word *malfeasance*, which does not mean quite what I thought it did, though in the same spirit I was inspired to change the name of S—, whom I have loved and now am forever apart from, this time quite eternally—she lives, of course—to Chuck, my new former boyfriend, having ground out the girl part. Anything to get further away from a memory.

I would cite all of the above as proof of my sound judgment amidst my day of medication and decision, but I have, at the end of it, been pushed further than I even typically allow my boon requiem composers to push me by the sight of the bloke in the bookstore with the outrageously oversized afghan sweater, frilly scarf, and granny glasses who protested I was in his way as I stood with my head pressed against a fat stack of used travel books, curiously located next to a fatter stack of Maeve Binchy offerings. He was in need of making great show of dramatically dipping his hand into the section labeled Essays, Literary and pulling out a book I imagine everyone has but nobody reads, a tired old joke I nicked from a courtroom drama on the telly, that day's cases having come to a close. And as in the back of my mind I have been up the river many times, I did indeed follow him home, as it was only five blocks, out of curiosity and a kind of lament, let us call it, and the boredom one tends to cite when one does not want to be alone without something to stare at—or a mission, even better.

Technically, I have returned from it, from there, from where does it matter—Barnstable, to be specific—to get, now, wherever I happen to be. And yet you must have a sense of waiting at the junction in Chichester to take proper stock of petty rogues and thieves and hellions—which summons up memories of contrast that are, admittedly, poignant, though I would not mind if such stuff were lost upon me. Or me and the boys, as I call them, which they seem to relish. Who await the command to perform—*Naxos!*—the hams.

Twins in a boating accident near the house, such as it was. Past stuff, stories and faces—your merry old uncle Dutch or Flam vomiting up his guts behind the local in Aldershot, one last time, a face in a picture book, my dear old Fauré in the corner, head wrapped chin to top with a dirty old yellow rag, looking like Jacob Marley in old two-reelers, broken-down men with rotten teeth from years snorting and spitting into corroded wash sinks after brushing out their bleeding gobs with toothbrushes daubed in salt. And my mother, for all the world, in the middle of an ocean. Even though I do not say it could happen to anyone, my idle consolation is idiotic. Opening the cans around seven and lining them up for when the call comes in from the west so there is no sound, none of that three-note aluminum business—the ping, the snap, and the whoosh—when I'm after another.

Having played a part in enough of this, for enough years, and listening to what I have grown accustomed to listen to, amidst tears, my mind does wander, and my memory is fronted with Chuck's refrains—who once accompanied me to the west—as the sound in the phone becomes more and more like a drone, and other thoughts, borne from the past, dreadfully crystalise. They always leave you. You never leave them. And now I'm one like the others.

Fucking brilliant that was. An actual mate, who is not dead, was kind enough to point out that such comments constituted, at the least, interesting observations. But what was I to say, my dear Gabriel whom, for a time, as you well know, I referred to as Gustave, and not Gabriel, as you are. I give you credit in your way, though some would say you meddle too much with your major keys. Mr. Fauré and his upbeat death dirge. And though your Naxos budget set is priced quite cheaply, it is not a terrible amount of music, is it, time-wise? But still, you have been many times a pleasant subject of conversation for me in the HMV classical section on a Saturday night, and I still prefer you—I suppose I always shall—to Berlioz, even though his requiem on the Naxos label is a double disc set, but still priced accordingly to the budget series, with a very convincing painting of Christ withering away on the cross on the cover that reminds me of a mad bald bastard I have since said several parts of several prayers for whom I saw waiting outside the city bus platform. He was all gee'd up over something, a crown of thorns tattoo on the top of his head resplendent with bright drops of dripping blood. On the same day, some spinster lady handed me a pamphlet, forced it upon me, to be precise, which I maintained was a sign, reading, on the outside: WHAT YOU MISS BY BEING A CATHOLIC, and revealing a man falling through the air toward a pit of flames inside the gatefold, with the words GOING TO HELL.

The woman across the way, with her shades open just enough, thinks she is getting to me lately, and I suppose she is, parading in her thong with her boyfriend, whom I watched moved in Saturday last, just sitting there, as the boys and I watch, clustered around our small table, Berlioz well worked up and demanding that the shades come down.

The scene plays out differently each time one is at the junction in Chichester, but what happens externally, what one sees, is essentially the same. Back in university, a mate and I would parade not so very far from the station, our dalliances at the local girls' school not quite providing the epic stories and material for local legends we hoped they would. Out one cramped room and into another, walls blurry and closing in, like they were toppling as we made our escape, a headmistress in dogged pursuit. A strategic stop, as if we were holdovers from a screwball comedy troupe, in a maintenance closet, where we sought simply to hide and instead were locked in, an overzealous confederate, me mate's bony lass, determining that such a precaution raised less suspicion that decorum and propriety—to say nothing of virtue—had been corrupted.

It was precisely once that this memory occurred to me while sat in the Chichester railway station, how the mad dash, as it came back to me, sadder after the long years, culminated in escape through a shower room, unoccupied, a general bath with nozzles on the wall that both reminded me of youthful days at the YMCA and got my mind up to images of the gas and the faces full of it. But on the outside, seated in the same hard plastic-backed chair one has sat in each time at the junction, different characters move in much the same way as the ones you saw the time before, all of the times before, really.

Alone, the last time, and what must be the last time, en route to a particular suffering bottled away in a particular house, not far from the shore, I beheld a fat bastard who voiced the word "great" and smacked himself in the forehead with his *Star Wars* paperback as the equally fat lady's baby, plonkered down in its little carry-cradle on the seat beside him, began to cry. Naturally, I thought the same bloody thing.

Moving outside to the taxi stand where it looks as though a cab has never been, and so a traveler, sans train ticket, has never left, one can delight in, as I did, the crude depictions of a man and a woman above the doorway, each for some reason with a perfectly round head and stick figure bodies--the economy of paint, perhaps--one swipe of the paintbrush dipped in black amounting for a head of hair, the orange and brown trim of the surrounding wall completing a frieze untouched since the seventies. And as I listened to a woman from the States tell a lonely looking man who was all ears, eyes agog, how she roamed the banks of the Mississippi near her home and there was a McDonald's not fifty yards from the pier, I thought of the last time with Chuck and the deaths, for that was why we were going where we were going.

There are people—and you, Berlioz, you pale, rageless sop, though I know you are harmless, would likewise agree with me— that one first considers fitfully, and then gravely, and, eventually, with more passion and less judgment than one is happy to admit. An individual who will only, at some point, decide they have had enough of one, and hail the appearance of person the next, who always seems to stick. There was that voice on the answerphone, an earlier one, pre-Chuck—from a time when delusions and necessities of expression get you up to making like you're in love—from years before, after first little and then no contact, faux engagements broken—working itself into a shrill sobbing sound, as though being coached, implored to sound louder and truer and more hysterical for people not known, dead, and a person no longer cared for. Me in the latter case. Twins in the former. A requiem of false feelings, and falsified grief. Not the real thing, which one measures against when having secured the real thing, and measures all the more, when that thing is gone.

You, Gustave, as the four of us have many times been seated around our little table, you and I along with Berlioz and Wolfie, the Mozster, the Big Moz!, whose requiem, from 1791, appropriately from his last year, nonetheless, is superior above all—we cannot quibble over your personal vanity in this matter—have admitted as much as what I relay here. You with your small glass of port, the Mozster (and who cares if Süssmayr and Eybler and Freystädtler had a hand) with some over-hoppy Oktoberfest beer whose name we jokingly try and pronounce (O the times Gabriel! The times we have had!), and Berlioz with his inferior Spanish wine bought on the cheap. And though it often falls unto my lot to make sure not a drop goes to waste, we have never been in less than perfect accord and agreement when we have stared up at the wall close by and expressed our thoughts concerning the Fragonard print that we nicked from someone's garbage—hardly stealing. That young man, in his pink shirt, with all of those white ruffles around his neck, perching in the brush as his fair maiden, beneath a statue, looks the other way—which really does capture her naiveté—awaiting his arrival. The times we have wondered what he will say to her—and in each and every instance, it breaks our heart.

And that time at the junction, waiting with Chuck, who knew nothing of the answerphone performance from her predecessor. And as I sat in my normal Chichester chair with my elbows on my knees and my head in my hands, mulling the deaths as I traveled yet again, for another memorial service, which seemed to have become biannual, it was after a while that I looked up to see that she was still there. Upon meeting my eyes, she buckled slightly, attempted to say something, the choke in her voice and her quivering, hasty gaze not at all lost on me, and excused herself to get a drink at the water fountain. And when she returned, she looked as composed and as strong as I had ever seen her. That is love in this life. It is that. Nothing less, nothing more. There is no more. When everything is for reality, and nothing is for show. When everything is for someone else. And there I sat, and there we were. At that point in time. Long gone now. Though this does not stop the racing back of memories, while I sit once more at a junction in Chichester.

As though there was not already enough to say for the gestures you can't get out of your mind—today, after surviving the crosswalk, after another night of videotaped trials on the telly, I made my way to the street behind Chuck's, and there crossed through an alley that allowed me vantage of her doorstep and still possessed what I deemed sufficient cover, for I am a back-alley traipser and an off-season mongerer. I had no intention of seeing her, or illusions I might say. The only point, really, would be to make a spectacle of myself.

One of the final movements—perhaps the start of the coda, to borrow a term from the boys—took place at an inn, in a small village one forgets the name of, a last desperate attempt to find some accord, or rediscover what is left of such a fanciful thing, between the four walls of a squat yellow room with faded photographs, one small, inconsequential museum and the vicar's house with its sagging, thatched roof.. And, inevitably, what happens is what always happens at these last-ditch outposts where nothing is reclaimed, and yet more, remarkably, seems to be lost, so that later a mate might cite that at least some interesting observations were made. One tires, upon the next trip, of waiting for a dinner car at a junction in Chichester.

Normally, Moz, the Mozster, as I call you between repetitive sets of *malfeasance*, I would no more talk this way than I would avoid your company after a day is done and all our dear friends departed. By ourselves with a glass of lager or cider, one can mumble and think on subjects like an answerphone and dear old Uncle Flam behind the local—if he ever really existed, save as some fellow in a picture book—or you brother Gabriel, not Gustave as I once called you, and drunken sops sobbing over people they have never met in long messages that lull like grey rain in villages with single, solitary museums one is not likely to remember, while back in the city one watches the thief make it running out the door with a copy of heartfelt, hard-won essays bulging under his jacket, scarf trailing in the wind. I did not tell you, my dear Fauré, you fierce bugger, because I did not think you would care. And you've my cans to open, you randy French git.

ONE-WAY ZEBRA

It was the day after Christmas, and watching Danny Splighter skate for the first time in my life was like the holiday was happening all over again.

Danny's family had just moved to our town of Belchertown, out in Western Massachusetts. This was his first practice with my team, the Belchertown Springs. Our name was embarrassing. Other teams got to be the Bears or the Marauders, but Belchertown has a lot of natural springs in it, and I guess the thinking was that instead of clawing you or something cool, we'd defeat you with backyard flooding. Or that was the joke my dad made, anyway.

I was one of our best players, but I had never seen anyone as good as this kid. Danny would cover more of the ice in one stride than the rest of us would in six. He was so fast that a single stride from him would beat six of yours.

His size was average for a seventh grader, but less than that for a seventh-grade hockey player in our town. I was maybe our team's biggest player. Because I was good and big, other kids usually found it surprising how much I loved to read. That was my thing even more than hockey. I remember in fourth grade I'd try and get my work done fast so I could read books like *White Fang* and the Three Investigators mystery series. You'd be surprised how easy it is to make a new friend just by recommending a Three Investigators book.

But my favorite book was this one written by Ted Williams about his life. He was a Red Sox star in the 1940s whose dream was to be the best hitter who ever lived. When he got to the Major Leagues, though, he couldn't stop talking about the individual batting styles of the stars of the league. He was so specific. This guy did this with his hands, this other guy's left foot pivoted ever so slightly as he snapped his wrists and drove the ball 450 feet. You'd think he was describing ballet dancers. But I understood that kind of enthusiasm as I sat on the bench and watched Danny deke defenders so hard that even our top players fell over.

"Jenks!" Coach Olin yelled out. Hardly anyone called me Todd or Jenkins. Even most teachers called me Jenks.

I hopped the boards and took my place on the red line. Coach wanted me to go one on one with Danny to get a better idea of just what he had here.

Normally it took guys ten strides to feel like they were right on you, but Danny was a stick's length away after two. He held the puck outward and back behind his right knee, and when I went to poke it away, he pulled it through his legs, bouncing it off the inside of his left skate. I tumbled over, and he went in to rifle the puck into the top of the net before our goalie could move.

I didn't feel embarrassed. Because that was the coolest thing I had ever seen.

We started to become really good friends when break was over. Our desks were next to each other in Ms. Pucci's class.

No one really liked Pucci. She was one of the youngest teachers, maybe twenty-two, and you could tell she didn't pay much attention to what was going on in her class. She did her makeup a lot, right with us sitting there, and the regular joke was that she was always getting ready for a date.

Danny and I had to write this little script for a pretend TV game show. That was a standard Pucci type of assignment. And I remember thinking, *This kid is really funny.* He wrote questions like "What is a tree made of?" and the answer would be "Wood," and there was this other one that went "How do you know if someone is dead?" and the answer was "They're not alive anymore."

Some of the kids didn't laugh at all, but I howled. He was smart, but you'd really get a sense of how smart he was at our hockey games. He'd be hesitant to get on the ice for his shift, with one leg on the ground, the other up on top of the boards. I'd have to give him a little push as if to say, "Hey, get your butt out there!" But once Danny hit the ice, he was a genius.

Pretty much everyone would follow in the direction of the puck. Danny was different. You'd watch him, with that amazing speed of his, skate to a place on the ice that the puck was nowhere near.

At first I thought maybe he was a little crazy. Here's everyone going this way, and this weird kid is heading toward the corner of the rink where nothing is happening. But just as soon as Danny got to where he had been skating, the puck would arrive there, and in a second or two Danny would have popped in another goal, or taken off on his latest breakaway on some goalie who had no chance.

"How do you do that, then?"

"Do what?"

We were sucking on oranges in the locker room after a game in which Danny scored six goals.

"Stop it, dude. You know what I mean. The skating in some random direction and then having the puck come to you thing."

"Geometry, Jenks."

"You're terrible at geometry."

"Not school geometry. Hockey geometry. Angles. Knowing that if the puck goes here at that angle, and then this player with that tendency does what he normally does, and then that bounce is likely to produce that additional angle, well, if you think three or four steps in advance, you can be where the puck is going to be."

"All that before it gets there?"

"All that before it gets there."

Before Danny got to Belchertown, the best player out in Western Mass was this kid name Brian Equale. He also had the loudest dad out of all the super-loud dads in the stands.

Some of the lines he yelled out were pretty colorful. You couldn't help but listen to him, even though you were trying to concentrate on the game. Like this one time he started screaming, "Arm the rocket! Arm the rocket!" By which he meant, "Pass the puck to my kid who has this awesome shot."

Danny was such a good skater that he was almost impossible to bring down. Guys would slash him, hook him, try to trip him, but Danny would stay upright.

Eventually someone would all but tackle him. He'd crumple to the ice and the referee would finally call a penalty.

When this happened against Brian Equale's team, Mr. Equale would go ballistic. It was bad enough that Danny was, I'd say, twice as good as his son—and his son was awesome, like, good enough that maybe he'd play in college someday—but that the ref dared to penalize a player for doing anything to Danny was too much.

"One-way zebra! One-way zebra!" he'd bellow.

It was a good line, even if the referee—who, of course, had a black and white uniform—wasn't biased at all. Guys like Brian Equale's dad tended to make for worse losers than their sons, but Brian himself, to be honest, was the kind of player who'd run you from behind at the end of the game if his team was going to lose. My mother said this was a case of apples not falling very far.

Danny and I started using the zebra line ourselves to refer to something that needed to change, but which probably never would.

"Do you think Pucci heard a single word anyone said in their book reports today?"

"Nope. You?"

"Negative."

"One-way zebra, baby."

"One-way zebra."

We even brought it with us to camp that summer.

***

That was the third summer in a row I would be spending two weeks at hockey camp in North Andover, at Phillips Academy, but it was my first time with Danny.

I liked seeing the kids from the year before. Especially Megan Fewster, who was the only girl at camp.

I'm not a fan of the word "crush." I find it limiting. Everyone has crushes. I'd had a few. Megan was the first girl I thought I loved, though, and once you think you love a girl, you can't say crush anymore.

That made me a little scared of her. Maybe a lot. Despite how well we got along. She was one of the half-dozen best players in the camp every year.

We'd all have to wait outside of the locker room for her to put her gear on. Then she'd wait outside for us, taping her stick.

Most of the kids taped the middle part, but Megan would put tape over the toe of her stick, even, and tape the entire blade. It seemed almost protective. But then she'd let a slap shot fly right past your ear, and it just seemed wicked intense.

The campus always smelled of fresh-cut grass. We stayed in the dorms, two kids to a room. The counselors had the same setup, with two of them in each hallway, at the very end of the corridor.

Except for one counselor: Loomis Cole. He had his own room, and it was always in the hallway where mine was. In my first year, he was what we called a "hardo" type, meaning he didn't smile much and he yelled more than the other counselors did.

By my second year, he was downright scary. He was seventeen, and big. Over six feet and more than 210 pounds. He also worked as a coach, because he had been an All-State player, and there were even rumors that he was going to play professionally in Canada.

The summer before, I had nearly kissed Megan. It would have been my first kiss. Her dad, who was picking her up, had walked in as we were the last two kids sitting in the dining hall.

When Danny and I arrived, I wanted to be a good friend, but I also wanted to say hello to Megan on my own first. So I left him unpacking back in our room and went to Megan's dorm. She always had the same one. She was sitting out on the front step, eating a muffin.

"Jenks!"

"Hey. Megs."

"Hey, you."

She stood up and hugged me. Her hair smelled like it had the summer before. Like cherries, mixed with that smell just after it stops raining when it's warm out. I sat with her with one leg crossed over the other. Two sparrows were hopping about in this patch of sand in front of us. She threw them a corner of her muffin. One sparrow made a feint at the other, who flew off.

"Looks like that one won the muffin."

"Yeah."

She leaned against me. But it was the daytime, and the first day, and I guess I sort of always just counted on the end of camp and the night.

Danny came walking down the path between the two dorms. I was glad he sat down, because I really didn't want to stand up. I introduced him to Megan, and he asked me what the deal was with the counselor in our hall.

"Why?"

"This guy, Loomis…that's his name, I think…just starts barking stuff at me. You could see the veins in his neck. He wasn't yelling, more like he was trying not to yell and that was getting him angrier."

"He's the resident hardo," I offered. Megan squeezed my arm, like I really should be nicer.

"He's like that every year?"

"He was worse last year than the one before. He's good, though. Maybe as good as you'll end up in a few years."

"Ha."

***

The three of us were always together. I worried that I might get pushed out, I guess you might say, on account of the chemistry Danny and Megan had on the ice.

She'd gotten a lot better since the year before, when she wasn't as good as me. Now it was the other way around.

She wasn't as good as Danny—no one was—but she was the next best player, and the two of them just carved up everyone else. You've never seen passing like this. They'd start way down in their own end, with a give-and-go behind their goalie's net. He'd shoot up the boards without the puck, and she'd angle a perfect pass off the wall that would click right onto his stick. Then she'd race through the center ice zone, get a pass back, juke around a defender, make a drop pass for Danny to collect, which he'd do in one motion as he faked the remaining defenseman out of his skates, firing a final pass back to Megan waiting by the post for an easy tap-in goal.

"She good," this Swedish kid named Magnus said to me as we watched from the bench.

"Yes."

"You like, too."

"Yes."

"You love?"

"All right then, that's enough."

The first sign that Loomis was going to be worse this summer was when he started calling Magnus "Maggot."

You joke around a lot at the rink, but coaches never called kids things like this. I think Magnus just thought Loomis had forgotten his name or couldn't pronounce it, but this wasn't lost on me or Megan or Danny.

"Can you do that?" Megan asked.

"I guess?" I offered. "I mean, he doesn't get fired or anything."

But it was Danny who had the real problem. Because as it turned out, he wasn't as far behind Loomis as I just figured he'd be, on account of him being fourteen and Loomis being eighteen. If he wasn't better, he was close. Despite probably giving up eighty pounds.

There were one-on-one drills where a coach would call out the names of two players and then fire a puck into the corner. You had to race for it, and either try to score, if you got there first, or stop your opponent from scoring if he did.

None of the kids could go against Danny, because he just toasted them. So Loomis had to go, and Danny usually beat him, despite Loomis getting more and more physical.

Danny wouldn't tell you if he was hurt, but after one brutal slash from Loomis, in a round of one on one which Danny still won, he skated past me in line, head down, and said, simply, "One-way zebra."

Matters got worse on the first swim meet day. There were two— one after the first week, and then one more the day before camp wrapped up. Everyone went out to Pomps Pond. There were three floating markers out on the pond as part of the swim endurance test.

The first one just about everyone was able to get to. It was brown-colored and called Serving Cone. After that, there was a bright orange buoy that sort of had these brown smudges on it that looked like an animal's face. That was called Red Tiger. And after that, way out there, was the last buoy, Black Rock.

No one made it to Black Rock. There was this rumor that the 1980 US Men's Ice Hockey team that had beat the Soviets and won the gold medal had done some training at Phillips and some of them got that far, but no one knew this for sure.

Everyone watched as the counselors tried, too. Loomis got the furthest, going a little past Red Tiger. And then Danny finished up for the kids, and went farther still.

That night we ate pasta in the dining hall. Loomis went around ordering us to have a second big plate, saying the dining hall would be closed most of the day tomorrow and we'd need the energy.

I had never felt so loaded in my life. Like I'd have to waddle instead of walk. I thought we were heading back to the dorms, but Loomis blew a whistle and rounded up his hall, which included Danny and me. He told us to get in a line, and we marched off to the football field, where he had us play leapfrog from end zone to end zone for a couple hours.

I didn't throw up, but a bunch of kids did. Danny seemed fine. Not a bead of sweat on his forehead. Which made Loomis glare at him all the harder.

That night I couldn't sleep. My legs were cramped. I got out of bed and started pacing in the hallway. Normally I wouldn't have gone all the way down to Loomis's room, but I could see the door was open enough that you could look in without looking like you were looking in.

He wasn't there. But there was a girl in his bed, under the covers, curled up and crying. Counselors weren't allowed to have girls in their rooms. I thought, "Aha, we have this guy!"

I didn't wake Danny to tell him. For some reason, I thought I should tell Megan first.

But it turned out she already knew all about it.

***

The next morning I walked over to Megan's dorm, but she wasn't there. I was thinking about telling Danny what I had seen when I saw, amazingly, Loomis and Megan walking side by side through the quad. I ducked into an academic building, cut through that, and made it back to my room.

"We could just look," Danny said, when I told him.

"Why?"

"To see if she's still there."

"What's that going to do?"

"Maybe she's really in trouble. You said she was crying."

"I said I thought she was."

The door to Loomis's room was now closed, so we went outside and Danny got on my shoulders and looked into the room.

"Okay. Put me down. Quick."

"Well?"

"Yeah, there's a girl in the bed. Asleep. She has a bruise on her face. We need to tell someone, Jenks. Fast."

I wanted to get away from that window. I also wanted to know when Loomis was back, so I motioned to the main door of the dorm and we sat down on the front step.

"You're sure it was a bruise?"

"Bruise, welt. Black as a puck."

"Jesus. I thought he was just a hardo. She's still there, though. Why would she still be there? Was she all curled up? She was curled up when I saw her. You don't think it's a dead girl, do you? And that's why she's still there?"

"She wasn't curled up. Her feet were sticking out."

"She's alive then. That's good."

Normally Danny would have teased me for saying something so stupidly obvious, but I could feel that he was in the same daze I was in. So much so that neither of us noticed Megan was standing in front of us, her eyes wet.

"There you two are." Her voice was softer than usual. Like how I imagined it'd sound if you'd woken her up in the middle of the night. "Can I talk to you guys about something?"

I stared blankly, and Danny nodded.

"Don't be angry"—and here she looked right at Danny—"but the other day I went up to Loomis after dinner. I was going to say something about him easing up on you, to remember that you're just a kid even though you're so good. I've never had any problems with him. And we sort of bonded that first summer when we had to do that tug-of-war thingy. And he just started talking to me. Like you can sometimes talk to someone you don't know at all. Or hardly at all."

"We think he's hitting a girl," I blurted out.

"He's not hitting a girl."

"There's a bruised one in his room. I can give you a boost and show you."

"That's his sister."

"Stop."

"It's his sister. Their mother died a few years ago. His dad started hitting her. He drank. That's why Loomis stuck around. Then she got pregnant earlier this year, and when their father found out, he threw her out. She tried to sneak back the other day to get some of her things, but he came home, drunk again, hit her, and she fell down some stairs and miscarried. And now she has nowhere to go, and Loomis is trying to figure out what to do."

I didn't know what to say. I said nothing.

We went through the motions of camp for the next few days. For the first time, I was glad when we got to the last night.

There was this skills competition, and I told Danny to pretend to be injured so he wouldn't have to go against Loomis. But he wouldn't.

Instead, I watched as he half-assed it, losing more points than he would have if he had really been trying. I understood what he was thinking. But I almost would have preferred to see a look of anger on Loomis's face, instead of the wracked, pained one that he wore all night.

He knew what was going on. Danny was trying to be nice, but he was making Loomis feel worse. It would have made me feel worse, too.

We had the last swim at Pomps Pond, but Loomis didn't turn up. There was a tradition of breaking a rule or two on that final night, so Danny and Megan and I snuck back to the pond after lights out, thinking we were being all rebellious.

We were pretty far off from the dock, but that didn't stop Danny from hearing the splash in the dark. I hadn't heard anything.

"Come on. That was a person. In the water.'

You could make out Loomis swimming in the blackness. I turned to Megan, thinking she'd know something.

"I think he's trying to go all the way out to Black Rock."

"He can't make it that far," Danny said. "Not that far and back."

My dad once said to me that a man will try to prove himself to himself even if that sometimes means hurting himself. I didn't know what he meant then, but I had a better idea now.

Danny had stripped down to his boxers and was at the edge of dock. I don't know exactly why, but it felt like when he was perched on top of the boards, ready to go on the ice, but still hesitating. I touched his back, with just the slightest push, and he dove into the water.

We couldn't see either of them after a while. There was just the sound of splashes. First, splashes made by two people, and then splashes made by just one, which came far apart.

I turned to Megan. "You don't think—"

"I don't want to think."

I could have screamed I was so relieved when we finally made out Danny swimming back, holding Loomis, who was sort of paddling with his left hand. Danny would give one strong kick on his back, and it would propel them over ten feet of water.

They made their way back up on the beach, and Loomis sat down. No one said a word. And then he just started bawling.

I looked at Danny, who was breathing hard. Megan walked over to Loomis, touched his shoulder, and took his hand when he stood up. Danny and I walked twenty feet behind them as we made our way back to the dorms.

Outside of ours, Loomis let go of Megan's hand, turned around, looked dead square in Danny's eyes, and nodded. Danny nodded back. And that was the last thing I remember about camp that year.

***

Danny and I didn't hang out a ton the rest of the summer. But then school started, and we were playing in the fall league together.

"You'll like this," he said to me, after his phone chimed as we got dressed in the locker room before our first game.

"What's that, then? Superstar got a text?"

"It's from Loomis. His sister is living with a friend for her senior year of high school. He's in Canada. Leading his league in scoring."

"How often do you guys text?"

"Few times a week."

I marveled at the way Danny played that night. He got a hat trick, his third goal coming with Brian Equale practically mugging him as he drove to the net.

Mr. Equale was particularly ballistic, and while I couldn't say for sure what Danny mouthed in his direction after that final goal, I had a pretty good idea.

"God you were good tonight, dude," I said as we sat on the bench and the final seconds of the game ticked away.

"You weren't so bad yourself. Four assists. Nice. Meant to tell you, by the way. Got another text today. From Megan."

This was odd. And potentially worrisome. We texted each other, but I didn't know that she did that with Danny. I tried to play it cool.

"Yeah?"

"Yeah. She said, 'Would you please tell your boy to finally kiss me next summer?' I said I would. And now I have. Wouldn't want you to be a one-way zebra. Make it happen and we'll start calling you two-way zebra."

"That's not a thing."

"Could be a thing, Jenks."

JAW BONES

His friend was quite adamant on the point.

"What you need to do is simplify things. You can't keep going at this pace now, can you? I mean, everything in your life is big, yes? Fast, yes? And after everything you have been through, simplicity seems to be of the essence."

He knew it was useless to argue with his friend. The friend had the good fortune of having been the tenth or so person to convey these very thoughts, and was aware of it, too, their group being a very close-knit group. Still, he was one of those people who regarded silence as an opportunity to talk more.

"Consider where you live now, for instance," the friend continued. "Right in the middle of a huge city. See? Big? Where did you used to live when you were happier? Small town. Sure, both were by the water, but you can't tell me that the ocean in one place is the same as the ocean in the other. There is a difference between a harbor and a sea."

The friend's logic could be slipshod. After all, a sea certainly seemed bigger than a harbor, but this was all part of his friend's method in working up to the end of his argument.

"And your job. Building ships."

"I design them. Other people build them."

"You know what I mean. Enormous ships. Tankers. Big. After what you have been through, I think simplicity is essential. Do the opposite of what you have become accustomed to. Go back to that small town, get away from your gigantic ships, leave the city."

"I have a lease."

"Well, leave it for day trips then. That's what my Carol and I used to do. When we did not have much money. Before we were married." The friend paused for a moment. "Sorry."

"There is no problem."

"Good. Thank you. I've always respected you for not being the kind of man who holds a grudge. Carol and I used to wonder how you did not get angrier. Everything considered. So will you go? Will you try a day trip?"

The man agreed. He took several to places he had never been, even though they were not far away. He went to the mountains some miles to the west, and to a lake some miles to the south, where he tried kayaking. But every place he went to made him think of where he had once lived, far from the city. It would be hard to go back there, but there must have been places in that town, where he had been happy, that he had never been to, not with anyone, and it occurred to him that he could go to them now and they would be his places.

"It was like I claimed them for myself," he resolved to someday tell his friend, who would surely nod proudly. Partly because he had come up with the basic idea in the first place, but that was fine too, so long as the desired results were achieved. And if there were places so close, to the west and to the south, that the man had never heard of, let alone explored, surely there might be a few such locales in the town where he had once lived. The best places keep giving even when you think you know them completely. He was trying to think optimistically.

But his friend had proved even a better friend than the man believed was possible. For as he sat on the train, watching the familiar coastal scenes he had passed many times before—those with the lobstermen counted among his favorites—he felt inside his right jacket pocket and pulled out a piece of paper which he did not remember placing there. His friend must have planted it for him to find. It was a notice clipped from a cheaply printed magazine—like a freebie— for a ceremony, in the town where the man used to live, involving tiny ships, after a fashion. They were rectangular pieces of wood, with four posts jutting out from each corner, wrapped in Chinese paper, upon which one could make drawings, or write notes, prayers, thoughts, wishes.

The friend really knew how to make his point. The man had never heard of the cemetery where the ceremony was going to take place, and he liked that he could, in theory, claim it for his own, although he was concerned that would be somewhat macabre.

"And after everything I have been through, I should probably avoid the macabre," he thought.

Still, how macabre could the ceremony be, when the news item said that upwards of two hundred people would come to the cemetery, gather at the pond in the middle of it, and light candles and send their lit boats out into the water? You could do so because you were wishing for something, or to honor someone who was gone, or because you wished for someone to come back. For any reason, really, where loss was involved. And yearning. The clipping put a real emphasis on the yearning angle, and this appealed to the man.

So much so that he purchased two ships from the gregarious woman who sat at a folding table in front of one of those crypts that looks like a door going into a gently sloping hill. Only, this particular door was open, and the man wondered if perhaps this was not a crypt at all, but rather some kind of storage shed, maybe for tools. He did not want to appear nosy, though, so he made sure his eyes stayed focused on the gregarious woman.

"Can I purchase more than one ship and candle?"

"Why yes you can. You can purchase as many as you'd like. We've had some people purchase as many as ten. Yearning can be a powerful thing."

"Oh yes, I know," the man said, patting his right pocket where the newspaper clipping was. "I think it is best that I concentrate my efforts on two lighted ships. Two is the number for me."

"I'm glad to hear it, and I wish you the best. Please take as many matchbooks as you'd like. We always end up with more than we need, and it is trickier than you'd think to dispose of unused matches after the fact."

"Yes, that makes sense," the man concluded, before he remembered to ask a question. "How many lighted ships will you be sending out on the pond?"

"Zero, for me. I find that I have all I need these days." She looked at him the way his friend had when he first spoke of day trips. "Sorry."

"There is no problem. I am not the kind of man who begrudges someone their happiness. Even when I have none of my own." He was surprised by his candor, but perhaps this was a simplification too, in keeping with what was to be his new theme. The smile of the gregarious woman at the folding table in front of the open crypt suggested that she would approve, and think he was conducting himself very well indeed, everything considered, had she been aware of his situation and his new approach.

The man enjoyed watching the lighted ships floating across the pond. They were not large—if you tipped them on their sides, they could have fit in shoeboxes. The air smelled charry, and salty, too. On the eastern side of the pond was a grove of pine trees, and, beyond that, a cliff, which overlooked the ocean. It felt good to be around so many people doing what he was doing, and he even made a point of introducing himself to the man who put out no less than ten lighted ships. The legend himself. He probably came every year.

"My technique is to focus on just the two."

"I see," said the man who dealt in volume. "I believe it's a numbers game, these things. The more boats in the water, the better your odds."

"Of?"

"Well, karma, maybe."

The man thought so highly of the ceremony that he decided to return to the cemetery, in the town where he used to live, the next week, even though the ceremony would not repeat for another year.

"That's fine, that's fine," his friend said. "See? It can be your place again. Maybe bring some binoculars. Maybe go birding. Think small. Order will come back into your life."

The man did not bring binoculars and go birding, but he brought a lawn chair, and a book, and he sat not too far from where the woman at the folding table had sat, although, of course, she was not there now. The crypt door was closed, and he thought that was interesting, and considered trying to open it, to settle, definitively, whether it was a storage shed or not. It turned out there was no need, for the door opened anyway, after he had been sitting there some time, and a girl stepped out.

"Hello," she said.

"Hello," the man replied. "Are you playing in there? Is that allowed?"

"I was not playing in there. But I suppose it would be allowed, if one were of a mind. Are you reading?"

"I am pretending to. Mostly I am just sitting here. I have been doing a lot of pretending."

"Do you make up games?"

"No. Not the type of games you mean."

The girl looked miffed, like the man had underestimated her maturity.

"I am sorry," he continued. "There is no problem. I do not know you, of course. I have a friend who is presumptuous. He means well, though. Maybe you could think of me like that?"

"And how would you like to think of me?"

"I shall think of you as an explorer. I was too scared myself to see if that door would open for me. And now that I can see that it does, I bet lots of things are done behind it. Is that true?"

"Oh yes. We could have a game of you trying to guess as many of those things as you can."

"Yes. A guessing game. Nice and simple. Let's see. Well, for start-ers, I bet the boys who live around here use it to hide in. Some of the bullies probably put the smaller boys in there to scare them. I bet it was a tool shed at one point. Maybe it is now. I was here for the ceremony last week, and I could imagine the woman who worked at the folding table keeping materials in there. Maybe even some of the extra matches. I bet animals would like it. Some have probably used it for shelter, or as a den. I bet some have even died in there."

"Oh yes, that is true," the girl broke in. "Bones are sometimes found inside. But it's strange—they're only jaw bones. No other kind of bones. Just jaw bones. I used to think it was some kind of joke. We would never find a rib. Or a head. Just jaw bones."

"Who is 'we'?"

"Me. And this boy I know."

"Oh," the man said. He had thought of some other activities that perhaps went on behind the door as well, but he had chosen to keep them to himself.

"You could have done better," the girl offered, having taken a seat on the grass across from the man in his lawn chair. "I bet you could have thought of more things. Am I correct? You know the kind of things I mean."

"Yes, I do," the man said.

"I can show you one of the jaw bones, if you'd like. There is one in there now."

But it had been a very full day, and there was only one train remaining that would get the man back to the city.

"Another time," he suggested, as the girl seemed to become older before him. He wondered if maybe he should have played the game more candidly, and if he was failing in his attempt to simplify matters, as his friend had suggested.

"You will look next time?"

"I will look next time."

"At whatever I have to show you?"

"At whatever you have to show me."

The man did not see the girl for almost a year, although he brought his lawn chair, and the book he did not read, to the cemetery where the ceremony had been, in the town where he once lived, many times. When the day arrived once more for the annual lantern festival, he gave considerable thought to buying his ships and candles in bulk, as that other man had, but when the gregarious woman, sitting at her folding table in front of the open crypt, asked him how many ships and candles he would like, he knew, immediately, what his answer would be.

"One, please. One is the number for me."

"Your number has changed."

"Yes, I suppose it has. I will take some of those extra matches, if you like. I believe I could dispose of them in an industrious fashion." He didn't tell the woman, but he was entertaining notions of exploring the crypt after everyone had gone.

If anything, the ceremony was more vibrant than the year before, and when the man returned a week later, with his lawn chair and book, and sat not too far from where the gregarious woman at her folding table had sat, the crypt opened once again. But it was not the girl who came forward, as the man had hoped, but rather a boy. Perhaps it was he who had found the jaw bones, the man considered.

He had resolved, at his friend's urging, to speak more candidly about what he felt, and what he was thinking, so he didn't wait long before asking the boy if this were true, if he was the person the girl had spoken of. But the boy did not respond. He was very animated, and even climbed to the top of the hill into which the crypt was built, bringing the edge of his hand to his forehead, like he was looking out to the sea beyond, searching for something. The man himself got up, stood on his lawn chair, and did the same thing, but could see nothing save vague stretches of blue.

Not all boys were cooperative, he knew that. He hadn't always been cooperative himself.

"What are you looking at up there?" he asked the boy, but no answer came, and as he squinted in the light of the sun, the boy must have run off, down the other side of the slope.

He heard a rustle, though—a pleasing rustle of the ground with a gentleness of approach, and a calm cessation of movement, as if one person has stopped in front of another they were pleased to see. He turned around to see the girl once more. Only she was much older now, and not a girl at all.

"Hello. We are here again. You are so much older, are you not?" He worried he had insulted this person he wished to call a friend. "It's just that some girls go very fast from being girls to women. I think it has to do with the kind of beauty they always had. You still look girlish, though."

"Yes, I suppose," she replied. "Do you think you're better at cooperating now?"

"Yes."

"And do you think it is too late?"

"Yes. To live again, you mean? It feels much too late for that."

"And do you know it is too late?"

"Yes. I do. I think. I do not know. I hope I am wrong. Do you know?"

They were standing outside of the crypt door. The man always had with him the matches of the woman from the folding table, for that time when he finally roused himself to peer in and take a look. It felt important to him to inspect those jaw bones, what had once allowed people to be themselves, to have their voices, but which now sat atop the earth with leaves that had been blown in under the vault door.

"We do not have to go inside for me to show you what I have to show you."

"Will it still be the same?"

"Yes. Of course. You know me better than that."

He considered for a moment. "Maybe."

"But we do have to go around the back of the hill. There will be bones there. They've all been cleared out of the inside. They had to go somewhere. If you have any extra matches, we can dispose of them. That might make things more pleasant."

They went behind the hill, taking turns sitting in the man's lawn chair, breathing in the smoke from the fire they made from the bones.

"Now climb to the top," the girl said, "and tell me what you see."

"You mean back where I had been sitting?"

"Yes."

The man worked his way to the top, slipping a time or two.

"Well?" came the voice from behind him. "What is it? What is there?"

He saw an enormous ship on the horizon, beyond the grove of pine trees. A ship of his own design.

"It's one of mine," he said, excited. "Interesting. I hadn't expected to see that. Not at this time of year. Are you someone I am going to come to know someday?"

"I am someone you have come to know now," she said. "But you are not going to find me here."

The man knew it was time to say goodbye and get his train back to the city. He thought, given his new way of conducting himself, that it was best to be as candid as possible.

"I can feel myself inside of you. Here. Out in the open."

"Push," came the reply.

"I am pushing," said the man. "I am pushing as hard as I can."

"No," she concluded. "You can push harder. It is not going to hurt me."

"Will it hurt me?"

"It is not going to hurt you either."

"I don't…"

"Yes."

"I don't…"

"Yes. You do. Just tell me when."

He figured, on the train ride back, that there was a chance he would someday be able to give the gregarious woman at the folding table the answer she wished to hear, and they could share a laugh. He imagined exactly how it would go.

"So, you have met someone again, as I had, and all is right, and the past is gone, just like that."

"No. I have met no one. It was more a matter of myself, in the end. That is why I need zero boats for hire this year, and why I can just watch, and feel peace."

"Isn't that always the way?"

"Yes, isn't it? I would be glad to take some of your extra matches, though, all the same."

"Yes. Please do. Please do."

THE GHOSTS OF THE ALLEY, THE GHOSTS ON THE WALL

His fears were myriad, but there were three in particular that gave him the gravest concerns: that he'd be found dead in his desk chair after a heart attack–inducing bout of onanism; that amoebas would eat his brain on account of the nasal rinse he had to do each morning in order to breathe; and that the girl inside of his computer who had left him was going to find him again.

To counterbalance this, he walked many miles in the middle of the night, long after the bars had closed and the last drunken people were home. He didn't wish to see anyone living, and the homeless people sleeping under bundles of discarded linen in alleyways might not have been people at all, as he never saw their faces. They could have been lumps of something. Lumpy rags. Bags of recycling spread out over six feet. He kept clear of them and walked at an even pace, hoping to steady his heart, whose rate would accelerate in his chair, at his desk, as his hand moved. But the more he walked, the more blisters he would get on his feet, and he hated the feeling of how a blister seemed to magnify pulse, such that he could feel his heart thudding in a temporary, fluid-filled sack of skin. Then he would lance it with the one safety pin he owned, heating the pin first under a match to kill off any bacteria, as the looming amoebas were already a threat.

They lived in tap water. He'd read about some people in the South whose brains were eaten by those amoebas because they hadn't first boiled the water they used in their sinus rinses. Not ideal for salubrity. He tried to boil water when he could, and leave it in a teapot overnight in his bathroom, but it could be hard to keep up in these matters when so much else felt overwhelming. Sometimes it was a calculated risk just to go with ordinary tap water when the panic attacks began each afternoon.

His initial interests in masturbating as his desk had been of a healing, healthy nature. There was his tendency to drink, for starters. This kept him from that for a few hours, and he could go a few hours working away at himself quite easily after sufficient practice.

There was his aversion to venturing out during the day, when surely he'd have to see people and could not pretend they might be lumps or linen. There was his aloneness. There had been people he'd been with, some of whom he figured, at the time, he'd always be with, but he wondered now if that was a case of trying to hope something into actually happening. They left with such regularity, whether that was after a month, a year, a decade, that he began to keep what he called his calendar-in-reverse on his bathroom wall. When something began with someone new, he began marking his calendar backwards, putting an X through each day, from December toward January, knowing that the person, for a variety of reasons, would eventually be gone.

They were going, that was one thing. But there came a point when everything shifted such that not only were they going to go, but the more he cared about whomever he was with, the more likely she was going to go without a word of explanation. Poof. Vanished. He wouldn't be able to see it coming, which made this person like a ghost, because he figured you can't see a ghost coming either.

He thought maybe the calendar-in-reverse might hold some clues, and he studied it under a black light, but it was only smeared with fingerprints and what appeared to be saliva but could have been the semen that was occasionally on his fingers.

One of the ghosts had made lots of videos before her disappearance, and he watched them in his chair, intending just to look for clues for how he might recognize a ghost in the future. But loneliness and desire would eventually play their part, and he'd have one of his multi-hour sessions, sometimes in tandem with the ghost on the screen.

This ghost took a long time to reach her climax, and she talked a lot during that process, talked a lot about them, how she felt about him. He'd listen for hours, wondering how the remarks of affection on a Tuesday could peter out into nothingness by Wednesday morning. He wanted to be with her again, be inside of her again, and sometimes he found himself leaning toward the computer. He listened with headphones on, the volume all the way up, so he could hear every breath. Maybe there were clues on a given breath, the way one went on longer than another, the way the next cut slightly shorter.

She'd tell him, near the end, to climax when she did, and then as that was happening, she'd provide him with one last directive to accompany her, using his name, and he'd comply, feeling like he wanted to put an arm around her for the first couple of seconds after it was over, then desiring to die a few seconds after that.

He could feel his heart really going during these hours under his headphones, and became concerned that it'd give out and this is how he would be found, and who would explain the nature of his psychical researches? He wrote the information for all of his various passwords—for his computer, his email, any relevant accounts—on the back of a billing envelope and taped it to the inside of his door.

He couldn't stop himself from his routine, though, and as inevitable as it felt—he couldn't, for instance, do his walks without thinking about it—he was not prepared for when the ghost started to move closer to him. It was only in one video at first, one he'd seen a thousand times. She was closer than the last time. She made her way up toward the screen, so that there was no longer any background. Her words were different, too, in parts, with more comments on how strongly she felt about him, what lay in store for them to experience together. If only—

She stopped on those words, climaxed, and then pressed some button, somewhere on her end, inside the screen, and everything turned black. He double-clicked on the file, and it opened again, just as it should have. As he watched once more, he saw that she was clothed at the start, which hadn't been the case previously. She disrobed, talking to him the entire time, saying that she had just spoken to him on the phone, he was working at his desk, and she wanted to make this for him to take his mind off his troubles. They had had a nice day together earlier, she said. Apple picking. At a farm. She had never been before. It was more fun than she would have expected. But that was, she said, because she had fun doing anything with him. Any day on the calendar was going to be a great day.

He felt his heart really start to pulse hard at that line. Luckily he had just lanced his blisters prior to doing his latest saline nasal wash, so he didn't have to feel his heartbeat surge through them. But conveivably the amoebas were taking hold and corrupting his reason, he thought. Maybe that's how it started. Maybe that was what happened to those people in the South.

They hadn't even been apple picking together, in the life he had actually lived. They'd talked about it. He had wanted very much to take her. Just like she wanted very much to take him to the mountains she used to hike as a child in the South. Maybe that was the connection. Maybe these were psychic amoebas, and they got in in other ways. Maybe the calendar had some clues. He hit pause on the video just as she had taken off her panties and lay down on her back with her knees pulled toward her chest. He entered the bathroom to stare at the pages, the clichéd photographs accompanying each month—an ocean beach with ice cream stand for July, a dusty sun-dappled glen with vermillion leaves for October—even bringing out the black light, but instead only smearing some of the pre-cum from his fingers into the space where some weekend from five years ago had already been crossed through several times by way of his accounting for the ghosts.

The screen saver hadn't clicked on during his absence like it should have. Maybe she had stopped that. Maybe she was trying to burn out the screen. Maybe she knew this was harmful for him, sitting here every day. Maybe she had to go and become a ghost back when he actually knew her, maybe there were reasons for her to do so that meant she had indeed cared about him, that meant she cared about him more than he could know. Maybe she cared so much she had found a way to do what she was doing now, helping him still, helping him always, like she was going to—

But that wasn't it. She wasn't on the screen anymore. She must have walked out when he had left the desk. He wondered if he'd see her walk back. There was nothing. He put his member in his hand. The pre-cum had dried like a thin layer of glue, so he reapplied some lubricant, and watched the corners of the computer screen—even the top, where the ceiling was in the video, because maybe she could come from there, too.

He looked out the window. It was long after the bars had closed. Long after the last of the revelers would have returned home. It was the hours, now, of lumps and linen, and what you weren't sure were people in doorways. So he went out and started walking, walking hard, hoping to develop some blisters so that he could feel his heart racing again. Maybe he had become the ghost. His groin ached, and though he tried to ignore it, the pain kept increasing, so he moved into an alleyway to relieve himself as quickly as possible.

A voice from under the linen in a doorway called out in a drunken, laughing way, which nearly made him fall over as he finished. "Hey mister, hey mister, bring that over here, what, you don't want some of this?"

He ran back to where lived, his breath barely coming at all, not really caring if he fell over and didn't get up again. Barging through the door, he flew to the computer. The screen saver was on again. She had allowed that mercy, at least.

With his finger twitching, he double-clicked the mouse. There she was, on her back. She was using a toy he had bought her. He put the cursor over the file and dragged it to the trash. As he did so, he heard what he thought might have been a rustle of the bed clothes behind him, in the bed where he didn't like to lie, because he thought even more of ghosts there than he did at any other time of the day or night.

He didn't empty the trash. The icon of the metal can stared back at him, bulging now. He thought of her alone in there. And he didn't want her to be alone. This version of her, if it was a version of her. Not even now. He had downloaded some books and some movies— of a more wholesome kind—and he dragged them to the trash as well, along with some photographs of the farm with the apple picking that he had wanted to take her to, and of the mountains of the South. With a single knuckle, he'd tap the icon of the can. Twice, like clicks. Sometimes the screen sounded like it was made of aluminum. But it never opened when he did the taps with his finger, as if the lid had been soldered in place.

RIMER'S BOOTS

In the summer of 1968, I was content to be working on the *Nabob*, a converted tuna fishing vessel that docked at Oakland's Matson Wharf. It wasn't the most glamorous job, and maybe content isn't the right word, but I was okay with doing what was asked of me, getting paid for it, and following the ship's one rule: don't ask any questions, and we'll all make out fine. We'd load the hold with some not especially large quantity of goods—which often was driven out on the rickety planks of the wharf by a guy in a pickup truck that none of us would ever see again—and dispatch it in Seattle, Long Beach, or any of a number of ports up and down the West Coast. It was light lifting, you might say, and if you worried that you were engaged in anything illegal, you could always rely on your ignorance to see you through, or at least to help you pass any lie detector test.

Some guys—it was a crew of three or four, depending on the time of year—got more nervous than others. Like Elston. He was from back East and used to fish out of Gloucester, going up to the Georges Banks. He'd lost a lot of crewmates over the years—four, anyway, which seemed like a lot to me—and you'd hear stories about how hardcore those East Coast guys were. But after the cops came around a few times to talk to our skipper, Reggie Thorpe, Elston would start chattering to any crewmate in earshot that we were all done for.

"There's our last voyage. What the hell we been shipping, any-way?"

Inevitably, someone would shout, between drags off a cigarette, that questions were strictly forbidden.

"Doesn't matter now, does it?" Elston would counter, sniffling a bit. The cop would eventually leave though, easy peasy, and Thorpe would order us to get ready for our next middle-of-the-night visit from a pickup truck. Soon the guys were calling Elston—whose nickname had been Ellie—Nellie, as in Nervous Nellie. Tough thing to live down on a ship of hard men, guys you didn't ask about their past. And if they were telling you about it, on their own, they were either careless or telling you for a reason, to get some upper ground on you.

I had come from the East as well. Boston. After Korea, home didn't feel like home. My dad didn't like that, but he knew how rest-less I was. We'd be on the back porch, and he'd be peeling an orange, in one piece, a skill I could never master. He was just so calm. And I'd be fidgeting, unsure of what to do next, if there could be any-thing next, or if the world, for me, was to be one succeeding patch of emptiness after another, a stark yellow lawn that led away from something—something almost too real—toward nothing. You just took that long road, and walked it.

My folks thought Uncle Hess's cabin up in Maine was just what I needed. Solitude, peace, quiet, all the pike and trout you could want in this pond not a quarter of a mile away. And time. To work on a novel, ostensibly, one which I knew I'd never write. That had been the plan, before the war. That's a lot of people's plan, though. And when something is a lot of people's plan, it's not an especially real plan. It's something you tell yourself you're going to do, but it's that hunk of bait—and maybe there's no hook in it—that you keep out in front of yourself, never lowering your jaws, never wanting to have its taste in your mouth. You use it for conversation, with people you're trying to impress and people you could care less about. And with yourself, a person who, depending upon the day, can fit into either category.

Time got awfully trippy in that cabin. Sometimes I felt like it was speeding up on me, given how one thought would become superimposed atop another in my mind. I'd look up at the clock and see that five minutes had passed, when it felt like I'd been brooding for five hours. My nerves were shot, and on the train back, as I looked out into the surrounding of forest and saw a couple pheasants walking with their backs to the track, I noticed that I was trying to gauge the train's speed, and that I was trying to figure out that rate to decide whether or not it'd be sufficient to splatter me in a couple different directions if I chose to come tramping out of that forest and step in front of it.

I got home and told my dad that was it. I had to go. I had to walk that yellow lawn and hope, maybe, that it would turn into something else, something more verdant, with a place for me along the way.

I cut all over the country, working one odd job after another. That can be such a literal term: *odd job*. I culled possums in a backwater Arkansas town where the creatures had the run of the place. I was a courier on a motorcycle in Tacoma and joined a biker club, thinking these guys, anyway, were as restless as I was, and maybe I could write some great ode to that lifestyle, once I had lived enough of it. I dumped gasoline on forest floors in Northern California as part of a controlled burn team. We'd gather in a stand two hundred feet above the forest, a couple miles off, and drink beers and watch those flames have their way with nature, satiating themselves by doing, simply, what they were made to do. I envied them.

Eventually, I came to Oakland and started working on the *Nabob*. I didn't fit in with the people you'd see during the day, in the city, in San Fran. It was like this hippie fest. Music was pouring out of every building, every car. Walk three blocks and there was no way you wouldn't hear what bands like the Beatles, the Dead, Jefferson Airplane, and the Stones were up to. The music was exciting, and a long way from what I'd grown up on in Boston—Shostakovich sonatas, Bach cantatas.

One night we were hanging out on the wharf, kicking around a soccer ball that a member of the crew—this guy with bright white hair named Cotton—had found. Of course, it kept splashing down into the water, and then we'd have to try and fish it out with a net. I figured the latest pickup truck was due in the next quarter hour or so, but it kept getting later, and later, and soon I was glancing toward the east, getting ready for the first rays of the sun. This gray El Camino came gunning up instead. Ugly ass car, but stylish, sort of, in how boldly it stood out from that weather-beaten wharf. You could have taken a black-and-white snapshot of those rotting planks and told a tourist it was from 1897 and they'd believe you.

Anyway, we'd normally handle the drop and start loading the hold. You wouldn't see Captain Thorpe, but he came racing out of the ship this time. The guy getting out of the car nearly hit him with the door, that's how close he was. It was a short guy, but he looked like he should have been big. He had this lantern jaw, a real galoot's jaw. No facial hair, which a lot of people had back then. Black jeans, an unbuttoned flannel shirt, a homemade Doors T-shirt underneath. I'd say he was rawboned, except he was too small, like he'd been shrunk down from some classic old school longshoreman who'd spit in your eye and then knock you on your ass. He leaned close to Thorpe and spoke two or three sentences. Thorpe nodded, and paused for a second, apparently deliberating his next move. He shrugged, with his palms facing skyward, and tried to show he was angry by stamping his foot, but I've seen more convincing performances at community theaters. And then he called my name.

"Clark!"

"Yes, sir."

"Drag that hide of yours over here."

I flipped the still-wet soccer ball to Elston and approached the El Camino.

"This here is Mister Rimer."

"Just Rimer, if you don't mind," he said, sticking his hand out. "You ready to go?"

I looked questioningly at Thorpe, who seemed like he wanted to tell me something but was unable to do so in front of our new friend.

"Mister...I mean, Rimer is a business associate of mine. He will be making something for which I have already paid him. A scheduling conflict has prevented him from delivering the product tonight. He needs an assistant. I thought you'd be the best choice. Given your background."

"What?"

"Elston said you were a musician. Back in Boston. Is that true?"

"No. I mean, I had a little formal training."

"That'll do," Rimer piped in, motioning me to the passenger side of the car. The inside smelled like antiseptic. "Don't fuck with my radio stations," he barked as we left the wharf behind.

"Okay."

And then he let out a huge laugh.

"Fuck with them all you want, mate. It's cool. Cool?"

***

I tended to think I was world-weary back then, a guy who had seen it all. I didn't faze easily, so when we drove into San Fran and turned off the main road by a dumpster at the opening of an alley on Telegraph Hill, with my companion informing me that we'd stash the car here—like this was a perfectly normal thing to do—I thought, well, here's another crazy, no biggie. You met a lot of weird people back then, self-styled characters who believed, in their heads, they were something they weren't. One old-timer would come down to the wharf every few weeks with a bundle of paintings on his back, cursing in Spanish and telling us he'd been kicked out of his homeland because Picasso had some grudge against him, given his superior skill. He was all right—a lot of seascapes that he said had all kinds of levels of meaning. The art critic Clement Greenberg was writing about him for some fancy New York City magazine, he liked to say. Fine, whatever, *buena suerte, mi hombre.*

"Are your ears ready?" Rimer asked, as we walked up the hill.

"Sure. What the hell. Real ready. Are yours? Your eyes ready? Your nose maybe?"

"You don't know who I am, do you?"

What do you say in that situation? Should I? You're probably a junkie. Maybe you're a cheap hood. Maybe you're a nutter. We knew this hippie who would go up and down the beach every day, smiling beatifically when he found an abalone shell, which he'd throw into this burlap sack \. As gentle as can be. Liked to tell you to love people as you'd like to be loved. Quoted the Beatles a lot. And then we learned that he went nuts on peyote and sodomized a retarded girl outside one of the local schools, and a dog too, but that part might have just been urban legend.

We got halfway up the hill. Rimer was breathing hard. He wasn't an outdoorsman, that was plain. But then he raced ahead and took a turn down another alley. Wasn't a trace of him by the time I got there, but there was a door. A small door—the top of it was at the height of my shoulder, and despite the Alice in Wonderland vibe, I figured what the hell, a job's a job, even if you don't know it's exact nature as you're doing it.

It was dark inside, and tight—the walls seemed to be up against my shoulders. The door closed behind me, and a light went on the second the latch clicked into place. There were posters from floor to ceiling. Rock posters, in lurid, DayGlo colors. The names of the bands, in psychedelic relief, looked wet, like they were going to drip onto the floor. The Byrds at Avalon; Quicksilver Messenger Service at the Fillmore; Moby Grape at Winterland. I heard a sound like an intercom going on, and a voice spoke to me from the ceiling.

"Well? You coming? Just keep going down. It's two more floors. Better get moving before Viachaslav does. He'll be pretty drunk by now. I didn't get him his stuff yet either. And he can be weird with his gun, if he doesn't know you. Don't sweat the accent. He's more American than anything."

So he was a nutter, clearly. Was it too much to hope for hazard pay?

I found some stairs at the end of the hall and went down a couple levels. I had no clue what to expect. Something outlandish or lurid, probably. Marijuana plants under lamps, stretching out in all directions. Naked women, even if that was pretty humdrum at the time. But what I found instead was a room decked out in stereo equipment, with speakers where you never saw speakers. Some were mounted into the wall, sideways, at waist level; others hung from the ceiling like stalactites. There were a few records arranged in an accordion display on the floor, and Rimer hovered over them. I recognized some of the covers; Elston was a big fan of the Stones' *Their Satanic Majesties Request*—although it was way too overblown for my tastes—and there were Mick and the boys, along with that first record from Creedence Clearwater Revival, local guys who were starting to get played on the radio in the middle of the night. We listened to their version of "Suzie Q" a lot when we were loading up the *Nabob*. But it wasn't the odd deployment of speakers and the seven different kinds of record players I counted that blew my mind. It was the dozens and dozens of austere, beige-colored, graphic-free albums that covered just everything that wasn't a speaker or a record player.

"Look, guy…I don't know what I'm here to pick up, but why don't you just tell me, and I'll start lugging it out."

Rimer seemed disappointed, the way an old friend gets when you've not shown sufficient faith in him.

"We're just here to listen, for now. We'll get started later tonight. You don't have any priors, right?"

He smiled like it was comedy routine time, but he looked sort of serious too.

"What?"

"You haven't been pinched, in jail, charged, that kind of thing."

This was cryptic.

"No. No priors."

"Do you have any prior experience as an artist? That's a stupid question though, isn't it? An artist is never in the past. Not a true artist. There is no prior, there's just now, and next." He selected an album I didn't recognize from his batch on the floor and placed the record on one of the turntables. "This is Blue Cheer."

"Like the kind of LSD?"

"No. Like the heavy rock band. Big lumbering sound. Loud. Sort of ugly."

I thought my ears were going to bleed it was so loud in there. Rimer walked around the room, checking his mounted speakers, sometimes conducting the music with a pencil. The guy was utterly placid. When the record finished, he motioned back toward the door and asked me if I wouldn't mind waiting for him for a couple hours in this bar across the street.

"You'll be paid, of course, for your time. Our gig isn't until to-night. Probably. You drink?"

"Some."

"I have a meeting. With Janis. Are you a fan?"

I was pretty sure, by this point, he was one of those dealers who dips into his own stuff. But he talked with such suavity, this total assurance, like we were having the most regular of days together, and I began to wonder if dear old Captain Thorpe was having one over on me, largely humorless guy though he was. But he probably thought I was too.

"Because if you are a fan, I could ask her to sign something."

He reached down on the floor for another album. It was Big Brother and the Holding Company's *Cheap Thrills*. I liked that one a lot, actually. It was loud—not Blue Cheer loud, but plenty loud still—and the guitars were out of a tune a lot, but that didn't seem to matter. It was one of those records that was everywhere that summer, with Janis Joplin doing those vocals that sounded like she was turning her entire body inside out. My parents would have hated it—they'd have said, come now, son, wouldn't you prefer some Brahms—but that music, to me, was the sound of what it felt like in that cabin back in Maine, when I knew I had to leave, the sound of knowing you need to light out. From whatever is holding you back. Even when it's yourself.

"That Janis?"

"Yeah, that Janis."

"You work for her?"

"I'm trying to do something for her. I'm not sure I'm going to be able to, though. It's a fine balance when someone doesn't want you doing for them what they need. But it takes all kinds of art and artists in the world, right?"

"You're an artist?"

"Yeah. Well, it depends on how you feel about the law, I guess."

***

The bar across the street was as divey a place as I'd ever been in. There was a neon sign in the one window that flashed the word Remo's, with the "m" failing to light up. The decór was what you might think of as dirty nautical, like Captain Nemo had some wastrel of a brother who went to seed and opened a shit bar. Fishing nets with flakes of scales in them hung on each wall, with bait buckets—maybe they doubled as spittoons—in all the corners. There were some stuffed fish scattered around, but all of them seemed to have had a part snapped off—a dorsal fin, an eye, a bit of tail. The swordfish behind the bar had been relieved of his defining characteristic. The jukebox was draped in fishing nets too, so I was surprised when the one guy in the bar, besides the bartender, hopped off his stool and dropped a few nickels in the machine.

"Really, Slava? Again? You said you were going to try and give it up."

"I am, how you say, in between. I want to like, but I no want to like. Sometimes one more than other. I know I should not like. But then I think, 'Viacheslav, who are you, of all people, to say what is art, what is not art? Did you not once listen to recordings banned at home? Think how beautiful they were. Did you wish you could not hear them? No. Of course you wish.'"

He teetered as he climbed back on his stool and downed the glass of vodka.

"You—why you come? Young man. There are better places in the middle of the day for a young man."

"I'm working for someone. I think. He told me to wait here."

Slava and the bartender exchanged a look, and the former nodded before pouring another glass of vodka.

"You wait for Rimer. He maybe tell you I have gun. Trying to be funny. Always changing everything, Rimer. What is up is down, what is wrong, he think right. You must like music. We listen."

Who knew that some crinkly, drunken Russian would be a Blue Cheer fan, but there were those massive chords from "Summertime Blues," the song I'd been listening to a half hour ago. Or so I thought at first. They were clearer now, though, even though this performance was from a concert, and those chords had a shimmering depth to them that made me think of waves of light. All we had were the shabby jukebox speakers, but it felt like that music was on all sides of me, physical and organic, as though you could touch it, and could not avoid being touched by it. I'm not someone to put down someone else for doing what they do, if it's what they believe in, and I guess Blue Cheer believed in being loud as all get-up, but this was something way more, like you were in someone else's head, with all of the pride, and doubt, that went into that thing they made that you were hearing. The worries, the joys, the reservations. When the song stopped, it felt like I'd been dropped out of one world into the waiting room in another, which happened to be this crap bar.

"So you have not heard Rimer's work before. Now you hear. No one understand how. Some say it is drugs, drugs in air. We all absorb drugs, Rimer put drugs in grooves of record. Some musicians want. Most, no. Too real. Rimer do not listen. Or he listen too well. Depends on how you think."

"You're saying he's a bootlegger? That's not so bad. I thought I was going to be running something hotter than that."

"Is not hot enough? I sleep now. For concert tonight. You tell him I still wait. He has money. Bad to make customers wait."

And with that, the beaten-down old Russian padded out of the bar. The bartender passed the untouched glass of vodka down to me.

"Fucking thief, if you ask me. I wouldn't want someone making a recording of me talking to people while I'm working and playing it for everyone."

"Why do you have the records he makes in the jukebox, then?"

"Why the fuck wouldn't I? People love them. They say he's a better artist than the people he records. It's fucking unnatural, but there it is."

***

I'd been sitting on the curb outside Remo's for a half hour when Rimer finally turned up. He looked more flustered than I would have expected.

"Bad meeting?"

"If you like tits it was good. She was a mess. Strung out on something, pulling her shirt up over her head. But she's pretty straight even then. Said there was no way she was going to let the label have me record her. Called it some voodoo shit."

"I heard as much."

"It's just my art. Nothing freakier about it than that. You understand a space. I don't mean, oh, look, it's a room. But you understand how the backs of chairs, their shapes, alter sound, and how the curves of the roof alter sound, and you understand what a musician thinks about their sound, where they're coming from when they make it. You put it all together, and you know that if you're at such and such a gig, and the atmospheric conditions are a certain way so that the bottom bass string does that, the snare drum does this, and you know where to stand, and how to turn, and you have the right gear, of course you can get a recording that sounds more like that musician, that band, at the core of who they—or, more than even they know, if they can listen honestly. People like live shit, so they buy it. There's not a lot of it. That crap Stones album with all the teenyboppers screaming from a couple years ago. Who listens to that? But live is where it's at. Live is life. Sometimes people don't want it feeding back at them, no matter how well they're doing, or how hard people are clapping, if that makes any sense."

"And you sell it?"

"Of course I sell it. Anyone who is buying it is buying the official records anyway. It's not my fault that my stuff sounds better. The suits don't like that. A recording made by a guy with his gear strapped to him isn't supposed to be soundboard quality, you know, which is what you get when you plug into a console in a recording studio. Some people say my work goes beyond soundboard quality, but I'm no critic."

It sounded crazy to me. I understood that fans would want to buy more records by their favorite bands. They went to their concerts, after all, and here was a chance to freeze those memories and bring them back home with you, where they could be reheated again and again, with the help of a stylus needle. But that there was someone out there who could view taping as an art form, with music that sounded different than you'd think a given band was capable of making—well, I don't know.

"Anyway, we got to get you kitted up. Make sure you don't bang your hands against any of the clothes. The microphones are very fragile, and they're all pointed in the way they need to be pointed. We'll make a trial tape tonight. The Airplane is at the Fillmore. I thought maybe they'd be canceling, since Grace Slick has been sick, but Janis said she's off whatever she was on, so we should be all right."

"I should probably phone the ship. I figured we'd have wrapped up our...business...by now."

"I already did. Thorpe's been waiting on some stuff. And since my last guy started running his mouth—and got shot in the head for it—there's been no new stuff. He said you're as tightlipped as they come."

I didn't know about that.

"Shot in the head? That's an expression, right?"

"Sure, if you want."

***

I hadn't expected that evening's Jefferson Airplane show to be the first of many that I went to with Rimer. It was a good gig, so far as my limited experience in these matters went. My job was simple, really: I was supposed to stand in the middle of the room, in a spot Rimer marked for me with some chalk on the floor, before the bulk of the crowd streamed in.

"You're not the music man. Don't sweat that. You're the depth guy. The crowd, the ambient sounds. It's a whole separate tape. Just do your best not to move."

And so I did. The Airplane was one of the bigger SF acts at the time. Maybe the biggest. Them or the Doors, anyway. They did their hits—songs like "White Rabbit" and "Somebody to Love" —but it was the more obscure stuff, like this extended cover of "Tobacco Road," that the crowd—the true cognoscenti, I guess—went nuts for. The bass shook the floor, and I wasn't sure how the band was able to hear themselves up there on stage, in that cacophony. But for me, everything—the band, the stoners, the occasional woman who flashed her chest, the couples groping each other against the walls— was secondary to watching Rimer. The guy was everywhere, crouching down, hopping in the air, turning his back to the stage on a given rhythmic accent, and then forward again on the offbeat. He seemed to anticipate every ebb and flow of sound, like he was choreographing it by the way he moved. For the opening verse of one song, he'd be in the back of the room; by the time Grace Slick laid into the first syllable of the chorus, he was in front of the stack of speakers on the right-hand side of the stage. Sweat poured over him.

"I think it was pretty good," he said to me when we were back outside, making a beeline for his car. "Lot of planning, Clarkie, lot of planning. You need to try and be the sound if you want to get the sound. Dig?"

We ditched the car in the alley with the dumpster; when we got to the door, Rimer looked around a couple times, like he expected someone to leap out of the shadows. The second we were inside, he practically ripped my flannel off me and pulled out a spool of tape. He had several on his own person, and, just like that, there was a stack of black rolls in his hands.

"Alchemy time. We'll see what we got. Should be good enough to fill a bunch of back orders. Give me a few hours. I'll meet you at Remo's. If Viacheslav is there, tell him he'll have his stuff soon. If he's drinking."

I was about to ask what difference it made if he was sauced or not, but Rimer was gone, and the door to that audio chamber of his had been shut in my face. I sat down on the floor to gather myself. Thorpe had had us do some strange things over the years. I was only two months into my second year with him, and I'd already had a stint at a funeral home loading coffins into a Packard at three in the morning and driving them down to the wharf. Elston said that some surfers had written it into their wills that they wanted to be buried at sea, which was normal enough, I guess, if you thought about it, but illegal all the same. But how many surfers die at once? Exactly. To say nothing of the odds of the lot of them insisting upon a watery repose. But like I said, you didn't ask, or you were out on your ass.

Whatever was going on here was less lurid, anyway. I was pretty sure of that. A beer sounded good after everything, and maybe the funny Russian would be there, spouting off. I thought he was kind of Zen, almost. But what wasn't was what I heard coming from the other side of that door.

That rush of sounds nearly put me back on the floor. I thought I heard the voices of four or five men. There were a few seconds of music, at an overwhelming volume. Then something would hit the ground, and something else would thud against the wall. For all I know, someone had been waiting in there, and Rimer was getting the shit beat out of him. Maybe he was already dead. I tried the knob, but it was locked. There were a couple seconds of silence, and a voice answered me back. It was Rimer's.

"We're just getting started here. Tell Slava we got a good one, if he's drunk enough…"

With that, the noise and the crashing resumed.

Slava was indeed drunk. The place was packed, which shocked me. I figured it was the kind of bar that no one went to except the people in the adjoining buildings who had nothing else going on in their lives. A sad sack bar.

"I tell you: show tonight, dynamite. I think Janis Joplin best singer. Best singer of blues by women. In Soviet Union, no blues. No women blues. Songs supposed to be happier, but happy song that is not really so is very sad. So blues anyway. But not honest. Joplin, honest. I play."

There was a pocket of long-haired guys around him, and a few biker-type women as well. They looked pretty hard, but a couple of them patted Viacheslav on the back as he made his way over to the jukebox. Within a few seconds, Joplin was singing "Summertime," and everyone who had been talking shut their mouths and listened. I had heard the song a hundred times, probably. I enjoyed it, but then again, the Gershwins wrote material that was pretty hard to butcher.

The cut finished, and another began, and for this, everyone who had been standing sat down. It was the same song, but a live version, and I knew, straightaway, that it was one of Rimer's productions. There was so much depth to that sound that I wondered if I wouldn't get the bends if I moved too much while it was playing. Viachaslav's eyes were closed, but I could see tears coming out of them, as they were coming out of a lot of other eyes as well. They were coming out of mine, before I knew it, and I didn't see biker chicks and stoners and drunks around me, but rather the edge of that pond in Maine, and the pine forest on the eastern side of it. I saw those two pheasants in the woods, I saw that train going over me, and my mangled eyes, one on each side of the track. I saw those fields of dried, yellow grass, the future I had set out upon. And I saw, for the first time, vague shades of green off in the distance, and those shades undulating in the air, in time, like they were dancing to the music.

The song reached its conclusion. There was silence for four or five seconds, and then Remo's went back to normal.

"You. Young man. You come back. Better at night, yes? Have vodka? You share vodka, so I stay longer. I slow down."

He had a bottle in front of him, and he dumped some of it into my beer.

"You should have your stuff soon. He says it's good."

"What you think?"

"I haven't heard it. I don't really get what he does or how he does it. It's all new to me. Way new."

"Is it? Or is it old made new?"

He leaned in close. I could smell the vodka in his shirt collar.

"He tell probably. Last assistant. I do. Not for music. He also deal heroin. And like you know, job is job. I not always do good job, but that is because of Rimer, I think. I can't help. What am I supposed to say—no more music like this. Is wrong? I know is wrong. Anyway, I no shoot assistant. Partner did. But I would have."

"What's your job?"

"Rimer no tell? Curious man. I customs. There is black market. Goods. Rimer know I am watching. But he say, 'Slava, if man cannot learn how to hear himself, man only a record no one play. Not alive. You try to hear, Slava. Here is what I do,' he say, and give me evidence after evidence after evidence. But I begin to hear. Even though it hard to hear. So I keep trying."

"And building a case."

"Rimer no care about case. Art is case. Music is case. Hearing is case. Me, I one case. Not important kind. You your own case. But you know now. You not know before Rimer. He know. So he not care about my kind of case."

***

That Airplane tape proved to be a massive underground hit. Rimer had a guy who worked at Elektra Records, who'd press up copies for him for a cut. We'd drive around town and unload them in the back rooms of head shops. A few cartons went to the *Nabob*. I figured I wouldn't be on this particular job much longer, but Thorpe told me to hang on for another week, and then I'd be back on my regular beat, if I still wanted it. I wasn't sure. I had this curious sensation of wanting to light out again, but for something more permanent, more in one place.

We were hearing that Rimer's latest bootleg was outselling some of the heavy hitters—stuff like Iron Butterfly's *In-A-Gadda-Da-Vida* and Cream's *Wheels of Fire*. The latter would stop Rimer cold whenever we heard a snatch of it.

"Listen to Ginger Baker on those drums. That was recorded here, at the Fillmore. Nothing to transport you. Music isn't music if it doesn't take you somewhere inside yourself."

He'd talk cryptically like that, but I liked him. A lot. I wasn't someone who made many friends, but I was getting a big kick out of the gigs we went to. Not so much what I heard at them, which was fine enough. But that alchemy—I was living for that, to hear what Rimer would come out of that room with. I never knew where that music would take me, what experience from my past it would reframe, you might say, so that I could see it better. With each passing day, the music on those bootleg records got older, but the more you listened to them, the more you felt like you were catching up with your future, the future you were meant to have.

We'd hang out on the wharf sometimes and drink beers with the guys, with one of those Rimer boots—that's what everyone called them—playing on the *Nabob*'s hi-fi. People would wander over from the nearby warehouses, and you could see what the music was doing to them, the first time they heard it, that it was taking them somewhere.

I noticed that the more bootlegs we made—it was funny how I thought I had some crucial role, like I was more than crowd/ambient sound guy—the less Slava drank whenever I saw him at Remo's. If someone put a Rimer boot on the jukebox, he'd walk out to the street and smoke his pipe until the music stopped.

I was outside one night, waiting for Rimer to finish whatever it was he was doing to a Doors recording. The Doors were his favorite band. He'd lecture me on how Jim Morrison "got it," by which he meant that he wasn't locked in one place, in his mind, anyway. "He's like a traveler, a searcher. But not like John Wayne in that cowboy movie. He goes where his mind goes." Rimer was no stranger to that kind of fuzzy hippie talk, but there was more resonance with what he said, if you considered it against the backdrop of the music he helped make. He was creditable, but damned if you knew how he did what he did. It seemed like it had something to do with where you were in your life, and where he knew you were. There were a lot of people in those bootlegs, at different points of their existence. Somehow he got all of them in there, like his records had an infinite number of grooves, and you got your very own.

I offered my can of beer to Slava, but he passed with a nod of his head.

"You don't like to listen anymore."

"It is hard. Sometimes, what I see, I don't like. It can be hard to know what person is if person wants to be something else. I prefer regular music now. Buy from normal store."

"Maybe you'll feel differently in the future. You never know."

"I know. You know something else for you. Just like Rimer know something else for him. And us both. He understand. I hope you do too."

Sometimes, when someone is upset, they want you to say something, or touch them, maybe, but I could tell that Viacheslav, in that moment, wanted to be left alone. Still, I felt guilty as I drove Rimer over to Berkeley's Community Theatre, like there was something I should have been able to say. An old guy, alone like that—presumably, anyway—having to look at what he might have been, and what he wanted to be, and seeing that nothing measured up. I was on my way there myself.

The Doors were headlining, with Quicksilver Messenger Service and the Airplane backing them up. We were, so far as I knew, there to listen only. We found our seats, and Rimer said he had to check something out, and to sit tight. I waited until the show was about to start. Still no Rimer. The sound techs were all done with their pre-gig tunings, and just when you sensed the light would be going down, they got much brighter and music started playing, although there wasn't a band no the stage.

The way I figured it later, Rimer had bribed one of the techs to play his latest bootleg, something we did at a Doors show at Winterland a few days before. I had yet to hear the results, but as I listened to that music in that hall, with who knows how many other people, I knew—and it didn't take any figuring—that I'd be leaving San Francisco before the sun came up again, with a whole lot of dry, yellow grass to put behind me.

But I hadn't expected to see Viacheslav, especially a fast, nimble version of him. He came running out of the wings, where Rimer must have been standing, because they both tumbled out onto the left side of the stage. Jim Morrison looked on, and Rimer got off the ground, without any struggle, and put his hands behind his back, where Viacheslav cuffed them. The music kept going, and I saw that Viacheslav was starting to cry, while screaming, in broken English, to shut that shit off, adding, just as loud, that it wasn't really shit, but it was wrong all the same. The music stopped, and everyone looked around abruptly, like each and every person there had to know if anyone else had felt what they had felt.

I was back East within a week. Elston rode with me. He wanted to get back to the Georges Bank, or away from Matson Wharf anyway. He said that the business with the bodies decided it for him, but I put it down to whatever he heard in those bootlegs. I said maybe I'd go with him, and make like I was Melville, but I understood that the only place I was going was back to that cabin in Maine. There would be nothing for me there, I knew, but I'd hear the place differently, and I'd hear myself differently.

When I got back to Boston, a month later, to tell my father that, yes, I would write that novel, even if it turned out to be terrible, he handed me a letter from California that he had already opened and read. My parents were always on the nosy side.

"Only light sentence. I do last job and then quit. Trying to hear again only right way this time. Even if hard. Rimer make records of this band you call Zeppelin and Van Morrison who is very different from others. I hear him well I think. Maybe I Irishman and not know. Someday maybe. Thorpe stop dumping bodies in sea. I tell and he listen."

LAYING SHEETS

His tongue tripped over the syllables, as if he were frightened by saying these thoughts aloud. He did doubt that he was standing where he was, outside of a familiar, stocky cottage overgrown with lichen and moss, a bank of nettles by the wall facing the sea. There was that old smell of cut grass and light brine with a touch of vague lilac, blending with summer rainwater over newly poured asphalt. He thought he had lost that smell for good.

"I really will get my audience, then? Everyone will be assembled? Everything? I can be the…speaker?"

She smiled back at him, so he continued.

"And they will all be here, and you will be here, and I can tell my story, and it will really be okay? And maybe we can resume? We shouldn't call it that. Fresh beginning. That's it. We can have our fresh beginning? And you are here? You are really here?"

She moved closer, apparently to receive his touch, but he couldn't risk such a grand gesture so early on. For if she really wasn't there, he at least wanted hold onto the possibility for a little while longer.

When she had gone, in the first place, as if she'd become an unearthly form of matter that existed somewhere else, he went to the museum.

He had to force himself to go, because they used to go there to-gether. He walked the halls with his head down, and the docents who made up the museum's staff would sometimes—gently, kindly—call attention to this, asking him how he was able to see all of the won-derful paintings hanging on the wall.

Sometimes a docent would find him in the Egyptian offering chapel. It was desolate—even haunting. The dead had been in here and now he was here. Seemed a logical place to think about her. As a joke they'd kissed and touched and groped in this part of the muse-um. But now he thought about why it was that she felt so immaterial, so nonexistent, even though she was somewhere in the world. Part of it had to do with the people to whom he now gave new names, who knew fractional parts of an overarching story. Witnesses at a distance.

For instance, there were the Breeders. The people who had made her. First made her, as he put it. In the physical sense. For he believed that people were made over many times in their lives.

And then there were the Remonstrators, the people she knew who did not know him at all, who did what such people do and ral-lied to the side of the team they thought they should be on. And also the Calcifiers, those representatives who purported to do her bidding as go-betweens, but he never believed that they cared nearly as much as he did.

Those were her Constants. He didn't have many Constants of his own. There was Signaler. He'd phone a lot and do his best to signal, through a range of expressions and arguments, that all, eventually, would be okay, a definition that grew fuzzier as time passed. But his main Constant was formally known as Sheet, though infrequently addressed as such.

There was a water mosaic not far from the offering chapel, and beside the water mosaic was a television that played a video on how this water mosaic, from Antioch, had come to be repaired.

"Workmen are seen here laying sheets," a pre-recorded voice said, maybe belonging to one of the docents. It sounded orderly. He hadn't known order in a long time, so perhaps he reached for the specter of it, even when the specter was not present.

***

Sheets in general had a high degree of flux. He wanted to have flux. A ship's sheets, for instance, had little in common with those of a bed. And they could refer, he figured, to the pages of a book, too, so that when he said Sheet, he also meant Book, which was apropos at the time. He wrote things and he read, because he didn't have anyone or anything else.

"Do you think I will ever come through this?" he would inquire of his Constant, looking at a blank sheet on which he'd like to write something, share his story, make everything known. He had this theory about death. When someone died, they learned what really was, who you truly were, what you'd done wrong, hadn't done wrong, and what they'd been wrong about regarding what they thought you'd done wrong. They had automatic, total knowledge. And he thought maybe Sheets, which were also books, could serve as the setter of the record, and no one had to die first, or at all.

The book wouldn't always respond immediately when he pitched his theory, but if he waited long enough, he'd get his answer.

"Well, you'll probably come through it, at some point," the book would suggest.

That last bit was disheartening, and the book—which naturally had motives of its own—knew that moping would do neither of them any good.

"Sorry," it would continue. "What I more clearly am trying to indicate is that I believe, anyhow, that you will come through it. Sure.

Let's go with that. Can't do anything if you commit to not doing anything. Maybe have a large coffee? See where it stands after."

The walker of hallways tried to buck up. "There's a start. I'll drink that down. And after, let's lay some sheets. Tell the tale. So all will know. All will be more right."

He knew how forced his optimism was, as does everyone who endeavors to trick themselves.

So he came one night to sit in his garage. Some light—too much for his liking—made it through the lone window, under the weathervane in the shape of a codfish. He turned on the ignition and pretended that he was a great pharaoh, one who had formerly walked the museum with purposeful strides, after all the visitors had left, before settling down in the offering chapel, a kind of ancient garage itself. But the book, toted with him always, was pretty blank. Remained blank. Where it would have been better to see a truth that anyone else could see. And the way death worked wasn't that everyone else knew the truth about you if you died. They only knew the truth when they died. It was just a theory. So he shut off the engine.

He took himself to another place he used to go, when she had material form to him: a beach with a cliff that sloped and might not technically have been a cliff at all. It was warm and he wished to once again smell the cut grass, the brine with its trace of lilac, the mixture of summer rain and road tar.

He lay on the beach, closed his eyes as the waves burbled, and saw a by-now familiar car racing around his head. He controlled it from afar as a child controls a remote-controlled vehicle. But this car, in which he felt certain he rode with her, even as he controlled it from afar, would pass behind other cars and mountains and long strips of cardboard that appeared to nearly touch the sun, and all he could do was hope for the best.

He lay on the beach, too, when it began to get cold. He shivered

in the sand, and sometimes, through chattering teeth, would mut-
ter terse exclamations that he thought worthy of a pharaoh who had
been sentenced to die—if that was indeed possible for pharaohs—and
wished to show a degree of character before his tongue was cut out.

The book, or the Sheets, or whatever it was, or they were, goaded
his imagination, because this was rather dispiriting, and it got neither
of them anywhere. The Sheets had a gambit in mind.

"How about if we return?" they suggested. "To that spot from
before. We could work from there, yes? You'd feel better about yourself, I bet."

"How could we work in there? The cottage has long been sold.
Do you mean for us to trespass? Sheet. Book. Whatever name you
are going by presently."

"Nah, dude, it's like the museum, but with memories, and the
mind, and you see who you need to see again, you let it play out, you
go from there. You see her again. You're with her again. And in the
time you're with her back there, maybe something works out differently in the meanwhile. People have a way of coming around." The
book was lying at this point, but not in a nasty way, though it was
selfish.

And so the two of them arrived, by the book's imaginative bro-
kering, at the cottage. The people who had bought the cottage from
them—he and her, as they had been—were not there, had never
moved in. It was empty, house as unwritten page. The man saw it just
like he saw paintings in the museum, or felt their presence, anyway,
when he looked at the floor, and he couldn't believe that it really was
true, the story was about to start, he could say anything he wished
and believed.

The car he had seen so many times while on the beach pulled
up outside as he worked himself around the room, preparing for her
entrance. He saw two fluttering forms inside the vehicle, white and

willowy, like bodies made of parchment, but the sun was hanging very low that day, making sea, sand, cottage, and road into a long, succession of whitish-gold forms such as one might find in a pharaoh's tomb, or in a fistful of lagan.

As he heard the doorknob start to turn, he panicked. The floor was barren, and, given everything, he thought it best to lay some sheets, just in case something went wrong. But no drop cloths, such as the workmen in Antioch had once used, presented themselves. He turned to the book.

"I'm going to lay you down, then."

He gathered his courage when he saw that no one else entered with her. Like he was gone, if that had been his form in the car with her after all, as he knew it had been.

"Where is the audience? Where are the Abettors, the Breeders, and the Calcifiers?"

"Here." She jammed some kind of small electronic device into his hand. "Pop it into your head. There's an adapter. They're all in there. All the people, all the feelings. Count 'em, if you like." She spoke as one would of dollar bills. "Let's get this done, then, so we can both be on our way. I do not have time for this."

He watched, dumbstruck, as she stood on top of the book, and her left leg disappeared into it, like it had gone clean through the covers and down into the floor. There even appeared to be a small splash of water.

"I cannot watch," he declared, and turned to face the window. The car was no longer in the driveway. He knew the room was empty again behind him. The book was the trickiest form of pharaoh, and it would get what it wanted, what it needed, to be whole.

THE TASTE OF SMOKE

Amongst all of the residents of the town of Living Dangerously, Timothy regarded himself as perhaps the least deserving of a nomination for the board of selectmen, which his friends had bestowed upon him.

This was a high honor, and it normally went to someone who had managed to add some new element of thrills to the community. There was, for instance, the town's war veteran, who used some of the skills he'd learned abroad to cut holes in the earth that were then made to look like solid ground, a canvas of grass stretched atop each of them, so that anyone happening along might fall straight through.

These inspired creations—which might have been termed hazards somewhere else—lent a verve to life, one the community considered harmless enough. To date, there had been few deaths, and those were relegated to the roads that led out of town, byways across gorges comprised of thick rock ledges, with slabs of granite that frequently failed to abut other slabs of granite, so that it was necessary to use ramps and levers to get one's buggy where one wished to go. The system was quite complex. You could say ingenious.

But Timothy was aghast when the honor was first broached for him to become a selectman. He regarded himself as a complete failure so far as the spirit of the town went. The forests were the real essence of the place, and he rarely, if ever, went forth in them. It was in the forests where traffic stopped as commuters tried to navigate their buggies from one ledge to the next, sometimes sharing a ride after a driver had managed to jump clear of a vehicle as it tipped into a chasm. Those chasms featured heavily in the literature cranked out by the tourism board. Considering that people made a lot of their own disasters out in the world, it might be nice to take a load off and have someone else—a place—do that for you.

But Timothy seldomly left the beach where he had built his shack, and knew precious little about forests. His shack originally possessed as high and flat a face as any seaside shack probably ever had. It was almost like a Georgian manor. But years of the wind lashing at that face had rendered his home a dully defined oval, with smoke forever coming out of the chunky steel pipe that served as its chimney.

Timothy loved smoke. Smoke was his cold comfort. It heartened the members of the town of Living Dangerously to see old Tim outside of his front door, gathering up seaweed in a fraying laundry basket, to dry in the sun or in a corner of his rounded house for use as fuel.

The smoke from the seaweed was white, and Timothy would sometimes stopper up his chimney pipe and inhale it as deeply as he could, trying to become one with the briny billows, and float away.

His contention was that, to do so, one had to be able to ingest the smoke, to taste and consume it, thus becoming consumed by it.

He shared this information with his friends, and they believed that Timothy lived very dangerously indeed, more dangerously, in his way, than anyone else dared to. Timothy had endured a loss, and maybe he couldn't face what that loss was. Or maybe he could. They weren't sure.

But Timothy was something his friends were not, and newness meant potential danger, which paid out handsomely in a town such as this one. For Timothy was someone willing to leave, and not just leave the town over the granitic roads. Timothy was prepared to *leave* leave. And this was very new, and it was theorized—if not strictly believed—that such newness could be awesome for tourism. Motoring away from the Land of Living Dangerously was frowned upon and tut-tutted. Timothy had really tapped into the spirit of danger.

"Would you be willing to speak freely, so that we might use your thoughts as blurbs in our travel literature, on your various goals and desires? And we can make you a selectman."

That's how one friend put it over seafood stew in Timothy's former Georgian shack.

"I could be persuaded, I suppose," Timothy offered, picking his way forward slowly, for this was all very new, the idea of anyone wanting his words for anything, and he felt like maybe, for the first time, he had some leverage. "I think I could be persuaded if I might be allowed to do what I spoke of. A long time ago. After everything first happened and you put me off, saying everything would get better. In time."

"And it hasn't? Surely things must be easier now, somewhat? You smile more. I saw you smile the other day when I came past in my buggy and you were breaking that crab open with a rock, not ten yards from where we sit now. I saw you smile, as surely as this urchin broth or whatever we are having dribbles down my chin."

"I'm not aware of smiling anymore. But if I happened to do so— and I know you've always spoken the truth to me—it would have been because that particular crab, who is not a land crab, had been attempting to leave the ocean every day for the past several weeks, knowing he could not survive. I simply provided deliverance for him. So he wouldn't have to be burdened by his choices. It's not often I get to feel helpful. So maybe that's why I smiled?"

The silence was uncomfortable, because the friend knew what was coming next. He attempted to beat Timothy to the mark.

"Look, if we allow you to leave by sea, that's going to set a whole new precedent that could prove...unwieldy. Most unwieldy. You get how this works. Living dangerously is one thing, and how dangerous, really, is it? People need some excitement. Gives 'em pep. But if you do this thing, we could get a reputation not for pep and excitement but, well, you know...succumbing and such. We want risk! Not crushed souls. You get it."

There was a great pile of lobster traps, dried sea mud, kelp, reed grass, oyster shells, tangles of mussels, fish skeletons, and crab parts that moved in and out with the tide. It advanced nearly to Timothy's door, then hovered at the midpoint of the horizon when the waters went out again. But Timothy's kind of beach was a technically a tide-modified beach, which meant it was particularly susceptible to the influence of lunar eclipses, and the one that was drawing nigh was the rare type that would allow a man like Timothy to get atop that pile of lobster traps, sea mud, oyster shells, and ride it all the way out to that point, discernible off to the east as a faint column of white smoke, which Timothy, and all of the residents, viewed as the source of the smell of the sea itself. A salty smoke so pure it was believed that to inhale it at close range would be to immediately join with it, a deliverance Timothy had been unable to achieve with his seaweed fuel and squat chimney.

"We could get an order and prevent you, you know. An order to dismantle that pile, even though generation upon generation has enjoyed viewing its peripatetic ways."

"I know you could," Timothy countered. "But I promise to leave your name out of everything. And after I write my note, I'll tear it up and bury it in the sand. You feel like you have to write a note in these situations, don't you?"

"What situations?"

"When you give up, sail off, and end it with deliverance. I'm not going to be killing myself here in town. It's simply going away and being no more."

"I don't know, man. You make some strong points. We'll table it for now. Eat your stew."

***

Under a sky that wasn't really of the daytime, or of the night-time, with the sun and moon simultaneously present and jockeying for position, Timothy climbed atop that great mobile pile of oceanic flora, fauna, and lobster traps, and set sail on the galloping tide. The tide was stronger than it had been in years, both in the sea and inside of Timothy. He'd have liked to wait to see what the selectmen said, but the time was now.

He went further than he had ever watched the pile go before, imagining that Neptune himself had attached it to a sled pulled by porpoises, with maybe a pipefish serving as coxswain.

The plume of white smoke once so far in the distance became thicker as he advanced, its mass growing outward but never upward, an observation which bled with other thoughts from an earlier time before he walked the beach with his laundry basket, gathering sea-weed, lost to a world that was lost on him.

"I am doing this for you," she had said, the person who had been his companion up until that point. "Not because I want to. But I'll take a drive, over the roads, into the forest, away from here. We're not both meant to live in this place." She said it as though he had built a world of Living Dangerously for her and her alone, and her time in the town, the one he had engineered, was at its close. "You will be better off."

"That's not true," Timothy had replied. "You don't mean these things. You are saying them to say something different, because you are tired of always saying the same things. Stay. Neither of us will go anywhere. We will change all of the things we say. We will say new things. It will be like we don't even remember our old ways, once we are past them."

She looked at him for the last time. "You are killing me," she said. One of the gaps between the slabs of rock, so common in the forest, less common here by the shore, under the mud, opened, and Timothy thought she had fallen through as the last word left her lips. He didn't even know people could slip out of the town, this world, in quite that way, but she'd gone and done it.

***

The pile had been breaking down as Timothy journeyed, losing a clump of mussels with one wave, two lobster pots with another, a football-sized glob of mud as the latest crest broke. There wasn't much to stand on when all of the energy had dissipated from the tide, and Timothy hopped clear of his ride, which sunk in three feet of water with a burbling succession of bubbles.

He picked his way to the shore, where the white smoke was. It emanated from beneath a bundle of smoldering rags and leaves, and was more sulfurous than salty. Looking back in the direction from which he had come, barely able to make out his shack, Timothy struggled to understand how the white plume had ever been visible to the people of the town, let alone regarded as the very scent of the sea. He bent over the coals and the white birch logs turning charry atop them and breathed in as deeply as he could.

The horn of a buggy drew him back to himself.

"I am so glad we built that over-the-sea bridge that the commit-tee had debated for years," declared Timothy's friend, one of those guys who you never know when they will turn up, which played well in a place like this. "And an invisible one at that! What will engineering come up with next? It is nice to find you in these parts, Timothy. The travel bureau just estimated that the real plume is out there, past that one, and that one, and that one," the friend continued, pointing, as Timothy strained his gaze. "Or that's what last night's meeting of selectmen determined, anyhow. Come by the house. We'll have some stew."

The man smiled as he said that final word, as though a shared meal of stew from the sea suggested the very essence of friendship. But unlike the day the crab had its deliverance on the beach outside of Timothy's shack, Timothy offered no smile of his own, knowing that in any town, in any world, in shared lives that become unshared lives, in pain's perpetual high tide, nothing ever really means what it seems to mean. The taste of smoke, the aftertaste of smoke, the hereafter taste of smoke.

He said some of the words aloud. Not that he necessarily meant to.

"Say, that's pretty good," the buggy driver said. "We can use that in the tourism brochure."